A DOCTOR, A NURSE: A LITTLE MIRACLE

BY
CAROL MARINELLI

MILLS & BOON®
Pure reading pleasure

First published in Great Britain 2008
Harlequin Mills & Boon Limited,
Eton House, 18-24 Paradise Road, Richmond, Surrey TW9 1SR

© Carol Marinelli 2008

ISBN: 978 0 263 86346 8

Set in Times Roman 10¾ on 13 pt
03-0908-44034

Printed and bound in Spain
by Litografia Rosés, S.A., Barcelona

She took a deep breath, forcing herself to be honest, hating the words she knew she'd have to say if she was ever going to let anyone in. 'I can't have children, Luke.'

And she waited. For what, she didn't know—disappointment, perhaps?

'I'm sorry,' Luke said, 'for the pain that must have caused you.'

Molly gulped. 'You don't mind?'

'Mind?' Luke frowned at her question. 'I mind because I love you—I mind because it's something you clearly want. But you're asking if I mind like it's some sticking point in a contract. I love you!' Luke continued, and as he said it he stared right into her heart, peeled off that last little piece of shell around it with his eyes. 'All of you. Even that bit of you that can't have kids yet somehow manages to love working with them...and especially that bit of you that would consider loving mine?'

There was a very big question mark at the end of it.

'I love you too…' Molly answered. 'All three of you!'

Carol Marinelli recently filled in a form where she was asked for her job title and was thrilled, after all these years, to be able to put down her answer as 'writer'. Then it asked what Carol did for relaxation, and after chewing her pen for a moment Carol put down the truth—'writing'. The third question asked—'What are your hobbies?' Well, not wanting to look obsessed or, worse still, boring, she crossed the fingers on her free hand and answered 'swimming and tennis'. But—given that the chlorine in the pool does terrible things to her highlights, and the closest she's got to a tennis racket in the last couple of years is watching the Australian Open—I'm sure you can guess the real answer!

Recent titles by the same author:

Medical™ Romance
BILLIONAIRE PRINCE, ORDINARY NURSE*
THE SINGLE DAD'S MARRIAGE WISH
NEEDED: FULL-TIME FATHER

Modern™ Romance
ITALIAN BOSS, RUTHLESS REVENGE
EXPECTING HIS LOVE-CHILD*
BOUGHT BY THE BILLIONAIRE PRINCE†
The House of Kolovsky
†*The Royal House of Niroli*

A DOCTOR,
A NURSE:
A LITTLE MIRACLE

For Marilyn, Jo, Delia and Kathryn—
This dedication is for you!
Carol xxx

CHAPTER ONE

'HI, MOLLY!'

Head down, bottom up in the IV drawer certainly wasn't the way Molly had envisaged meeting Luke again.

Years ago, she'd sworn that if their paths should ever cross again she'd be thin, thin, thin, and wearing some strappy little black number, with her wild curly brown hair for once all sleek and straightened, sipping champagne—at a party, perhaps, with a gorgeous, *doting* man on her arm, laughing together at some intimate joke.... Oh, and she'd frown, just a tiny little frown as, for a second or two, she tried to place him...

'Oh, hi, Luke!'

Blushing, pulling down her top to cover her less-than-skinny bottom as she stood, Molly managed not one of the above aims.

She'd heard he was back in Melbourne—had heard the terrible news about his wife, and had sort of wondered if he'd come back to Melbourne Central—but really her mind had been too full of other things to dwell on it.

'How are you, Molly?' His voice was as deep as ever and he looked the same—sort of.

Still taller than most, still blonder than most, those green eyes still gorgeous and that voice still incredibly crisp—only he looked older.

Not fat, balding, beer-gut older.

Just…her chocolate-brown eyes scrutinised his face for a second before she answered…tired, Molly almost decided, then changed her mind. Sad, perhaps, but that didn't quite fit either.

'I'm well, thanks.' So much for some sparkling, witty reply! 'And you?'

'Not bad.'

Of all the stupid questions to ask. Molly could have kicked herself, but instead she took a deep breath and tried to repeat the words she'd offered in the card she'd sent him six months ago.

'I was so sorry to hear…' Her voice faltered. It was easier to write it than say it. On second thoughts, even writing it hadn't been that easy—it had taken five cards and about a week of drafts to come up with her rather paltry offering.

Dear Luke,
I heard the terrible news about Amanda at work.
I am so sorry for your loss.
So sorry for the twins' loss, too.
Am thinking of you all.
Molly (Hampton née Jones, Children's Ward at Melbourne Central)

'How are you all coping?' she settled for instead.
'Getting there—slowly.' Luke shrugged. 'It's good to

be back in Melbourne, having my family here and everything.'

'And how are the twins?'

'Getting there, too,' Luke gave another tight shrug, 'though, very slowly. Anyway, enough about me—how are you doing, Molly *Hampton*? Belated congratulations, by the way.'

'Extremely belated…' Molly took a deep breath, always horribly awkward at this bit, and she was almost saved from saying it as around the same time she spoke his eyes dragged down to her name badge. 'It's actually Molly Jones again.'

'Ouch.' He gave a tiny wince. 'Since when?'

'Since a couple of weeks ago. We broke up last year, but the divorce just came through. I figured the time was right to change my name back.'

'I'm sorry to hear that. Any kids?'

'None.'

'Well, that's good.' Luke smiled, unwittingly turning the knife.

'It is…' Molly fished for her mask, that smiling mask she wore quite often. 'It makes things a lot less complicated.'

Only it didn't.

The fact that there were no children was the reason she was minus a wedding ring.

Not that he needed to know.

Not that he'd understand.

'Well, I'm very sorry,' Luke concluded, because he'd gone to private school, because somehow he always remembered his manners, 'for all that you've been through.'

'Let's both stop saying sorry, huh?' Molly suggested, and Luke smiled again.

Smiled because it was Molly.

Smiled because somehow, in a matter of seconds, she'd waved the barriers away.

'So how are you—really?' Luke probed, moving past the niceties and getting to the point.

'Getting there,' Molly answered, then her smile widened, 'Well, I've read every self-help book in the library and I just did a quiz in a magazine and apparently I'm "a woman in control" so I'd say I *am* just about there! So what are you doing now—registrar, consultant…?'

'Heavens, no.' Luke shook his head. 'There's a registrar position coming up here that I've applied for—I'm just filling in to cover annual leave as a resident for now—and they've lumbered me with a month of nights.' He must have seen her frown. Five years ago it would have made sense—five years ago Luke had been coming to the end of his paediatric rotation; five years ago he would have been starting to apply for a registrar's position—but now? It didn't make sense, and Luke filled in the silence with an explanation. 'With the twins and everything, I had a crazy idea of being a GP—well, that was the plan. I started doing some shifts at a local walk-in, walk-out clinic to see if I'd like it and, well, the money and the hours were good.'

Since when had Luke cared about the money or the hours? Luke Williams had lived and breathed paediatrics—would have done it for nothing in Molly's opinion. Not that he wanted her opinion, she reminded herself—not that he wanted her. Luke had made that stunningly clear five years ago.

Five years almost to the day, in fact.

When he'd walked into the café and after a few choice words had walked out of her life.

Walked out on *them* as he'd run back to Amanda.

'Are you ready to check the IVs, Molly?' her colleague Anne Marie called out. 'Rita wants to start handover.'

'Coming.'

'So you're doing a stint of nights, too?' Luke asked as they both headed down to the cots area.

'I do permanent nights now. There was an ACN position and I decided to give it a go.'

'You're an associate charge nurse?' She could hear the surprise in his voice and didn't blame him—the Molly Jones of five years ago couldn't have cared less about promotions and the like, and Saturday nights had been for dancing! 'You've done well—you really are a woman in control!'

'Thanks. Well, it's good to see you,' Molly said. 'I'd better go—I want to check all the IVs before handover. No doubt I'll see you soon.'

'No doubt.'

Molly always checked the IVs before handover, hated them bleeping and going off during it—hated the day staff leaving and then finding out there was a query with an order or rate and having to ring them at home. And it made handover a lot easier if she had at least glimpsed the patients. It was just something she did and usually very quickly—only not tonight.

Tonight the IV round took for ever, Molly having to check and recheck everything, reeling, just reeling, at having seen Luke again. She'd wondered how she'd feel if she saw him again. When she'd heard that he'd moved back, Molly had wondered if, after all these years, after all that had happened, he'd have any effect on her—had convinced herself almost that the intense feelings she'd had for him all those years ago had been nothing more than a crush.

Some crush!

Her mind whirred back to that dangerous place.

When life had been just about perfect.

When for three months, three glorious and passion-filled months, she'd held him—and been held by him.

Had lain in his arms and been kissed.

Had kissed him back without reservation—safe in the knowledge, that this wonderful, breathtaking man was as into her as she was into him.

Had given every little piece of herself, because she'd *known* he was worth it.

'Did you not sleep today?' Anne Marie's Scottish accent was, Molly was sure, as broad as it had been the on the day she'd landed in Australia twenty years ago!

'I had a great sleep.'

'She's miles away!' Anne Marie winked at Bernadette, a twelve-year-old who'd been on the children's ward for three weeks now with osteomyelitis—a particularly nasty bone disease, which in this case affected Bernadette's femur. Despite rigorous treatment that had required not just IV antibiotics but surgical intervention too, it was a long slow process to get her better, and the young girl was going to be on the ward for quite a while yet. 'Molly's off in a dream world of her own,' Anne Marie carried on, but not even Anne Marie's good-natured jesting could raise a smile from Bernadette tonight.

Still, her mind wasn't on Luke or anything other than

work when they came to cot four. Rita, the charge nurse for the day, was exchanging a frown with Molly that didn't bode well, while talking reassuringly to the baby's mother. 'I'm going to ask Dr Williams to come and have another look at Declan. Amy…' Rita turned to one of the day staff '…could you stay with Declan while I give handover? Give us a call if you're concerned.'

'I'm not happy with that little one,' Rita continued once she'd spoken to Luke and they were in handover. 'He's going to be taking up a lot of your night. Declan Edwards, eight weeks, born at thirty-six weeks gestation so a touch prem, was admitted at lunchtime with bronchiolitis and he was doing well till a little while ago—IV fluids, oxygen, minimal handling—but his O2 sats have started to drop. I called Tom, the resident, and he had another look at him an hour or so ago and we increased the oxygen rate, but he's still struggling. I'm glad Luke's just come on, actually…'

Handover on a children's ward was always long and detailed, with not just the children but their families to discuss and endless reams of tiny information that might be relevant at two in the morning when a two-year-old was crying out for his purple bear or, as in tonight's case, a normally happy twelve-year-old whose mood had suddenly changed.

'Bernadette's been pretty low this evening,' Rita said as they came to their last patient at handover, 'which is to be expected, given the length of time she's been here, but she was fine right up until lunchtime. She's had lots of visitors, though. She might just be having a quiet night.'

'No, I noticed she seemed pretty flat when I checked the drips,' Molly agreed.

'All the children in her bay have been discharged so maybe she's feeling a bit lonely. I've told her that we'll soon fill up, and Mum spoke to her before she went home, but she says she's OK, just tired. I don't want to nag her. Everyone's entitled to an off day!'

'It's just not like her, though, is it?' Anne Marie said. 'She's such a bubbly, happy wee thing.'

'We'll keep an eye on her.' Molly didn't bother to write it down, neither did Anne Marie. Both knew their patient well enough not to need reminding.

'Well, I hope you have a good night,' Rita said, handing over the keys to Molly, 'though I think Declan's going to keep you busy. Still, it's good that Luke's on—I can't believe he's just a resident! You remember Luke…' Rita trailed off, obviously having just remembered that Molly would remember Luke Williams rather well. But even though she didn't elaborate, that was all it took for Anne Marie to pounce the second Molly had allocated the staff and was pulling the drug trolley out.

'So!'

'So, what?' Molly blushed.

'That dishy doctor you were talking to before hand-over—why would *you* remember him?'

'Because he used to work here.' Molly shrugged. 'Before your time.'

'Before Richard's time?' Anne Marie asked perceptively, barring Molly's access to the door. 'When you were young free and single, perhaps?'

'Perhaps!' Molly said tightly, pushing forward, deciding that if Anne Marie didn't move, she'd just run her over with the drug trolley, but Anne Marie stood back, smirking as Molly bulldozed past. 'Hey, Molly.' Anne Marie tapped her shoulder. 'You still are!'

'Are what?' Molly frowned. 'Am what?'

'Young, free and single.'

'Wrong…' Molly gave wry smile, strangely close to tears all of a sudden. 'I'm older, wiser and very newly divorced. Believe me, Luke Williams is absolutely the *last* thing I need right now!'

Though it *was* good to have him on duty tonight.

Good, because a poor excuse for a boyfriend he might have once been but he was an excellent doctor.

Young Declan had Molly suitably on edge and even though Anne Marie was looking after him, the drug trolley was quickly locked and put away, when Anne Marie called Molly over to say that even during handover his condition had deteriorated. His rapid respiration and heart-rate, combined with nasal flaring, indicating he was struggling, despite the oxygen tent he was in.

'Where's his mum?' Luke asked as Molly came in with a head box which would deliver a higher concentration of oxygen to the infant as Anne Marie spoke on the phone.

'She's in the parents' room, ringing Declan's dad. I told her to have a coffee and that you'd come and talk to her soon.'

'Where the hell's Doug?' Luke whistled through his teeth as he urged his consultant to suddenly appear. 'I rang him half an hour ago—he should be here by now.'

'Do you want me to page the anaesthetist?'

'I've paged him.' Anne Marie gave a tight smile.

'Twice. He's stuck down in Emergency and we're waiting for the second one to finish up in theatre.'

And whoever thought night shift was about sitting at the desk and guzzling chocolate had never done it.

Had never worked night after night with skeleton staff and patients that were just as sick at night as during the day, only without the resources to match it. With Molly and Anne Marie tied up with Declan, the ward was being watched by Louanna, a division two nurse, and Debbie the Grad. Most of the senior medical staff had long since gone home and the ones that were here at the hospital were clearly tied up elsewhere.

There was a thin line between a sick baby and a really sick one, and as Luke picked up one floppy, mottled leg, Molly knew Declan was crossing it.

'Ring ICU,' Luke said.

'There isn't a cot,' Molly said, because she'd already checked. 'There will be in an hour or so.'

'Get them on the phone for me.'

Which she did.

And Luke explained in no uncertain terms to a unit that was being run ragged that unless they cleared a space soon, they'd be running to answer a crash call.

'Making enemies, Luke?' Doug Evans, wearing shorts and T-shirt and hauled away from wherever he'd been, looked nothing like the paediatric consultant he was. He was an extremely nice doctor and a very diligent one, too, and everyone, except Declan, breathed a bit more easily as soon as he arrived.

He examined the little babe gently as Luke gave his boss the background.

'I just want some blood gases and then we'd better get him over to ICU. Thanks…' he glanced over to Luke '…for calling me in.'

'Always happy to see you, Doug!' Luke gave a tight smile. 'Molly, can you come and talk to the mum with me?'

And the dad!

Having raced along the corridor, Mr Edwards burst into the ward, his eyes shocked when he saw his son, especially as at that moment Doug happened to be sticking in a needle to do a quick set of blood gases.

'What's that? What's going on?'

'That's called a head box,' Luke said calmly. 'It's to give your son a higher concentration of oxygen and we're just taking some blood gases. I'm Dr Williams. I was just about to talk to your wife, if you'd like to come down to the—'

'I'm staying here!' Mr Edwards barked. 'You can tell me what's going on here.'

'No, I can't,' Luke answered easily. 'Declan needs rest and to be kept quiet and I don't want any tension around him.'

'I'm fine! I just want to know what's going on.'

'Well, come down to the parents' room and I'll tell you, along with your wife.' And without further word he turned and walked out, politely, calmly, but making it absolutely clear he wasn't going to change his mind. And after a very short time, Mr Edwards followed.

'Wow!' Anne Marie gawked in admiration. 'I'm going to *like* working with Luke Williams. Off you go!'

'Press the bell if you need me.'

'Sure.'

Lucy Edwards was very different in nature from her

husband—a calm woman, she actually seemed relieved when Luke explained that their son was going to be transferred to the intensive care unit.

'But he was fine when I left.' Mr Edwards looked appalled. 'I want to know what the hell happened.'

'He just suddenly got worse, Mike.'

'Why?' Mike said accusingly. 'You're supposed to get better in hospital.'

'And he will,' Luke said firmly. 'But bronchiolitis, especially in such a small baby, often gets worse before it gets better—and your son needs more monitoring and support than we can adequately give him down here on the ward. He needs one-on-one nursing, and if he does deteriorate further I'd far rather he was already in Intensive Care, with doctors and an anaesthetist to hand, than have us putting out an emergency call at two in the morning.'

'But he'll be OK…?'

'With the right treatment and the right care,' Luke said calmly, 'which is what he'll get in Intensive Care, where he should do well.'

'He will be OK?' It was Lucy asking now, tears and fear starting to catch up with her, and though no one could guarantee anything, Luke's quiet assurance was what was needed. 'He just seems so tiny…'

'He's struggling right now,' Luke agreed, 'and the next twenty-four to forty-eight hours are going to be difficult, but I fully expect him back on the ward with us in a couple of days. The best thing we can do now is get him moved up there, get him settled.'

He made it all so straightforward—he always had, Molly realised as within half an hour she had resumed the drug round as a little entourage trooped to ICU with their precious cargo. Utterly confident in his own decisions, and utterly willing to admit when he couldn't work miracles, he'd never been one to waste time calling in help or transferring a sick child.

But that was Luke, Molly thought with a mental sigh as she added some antibiotics to Bernadette's flask and upped the rate—decisive, straight to the point.

And when he decided he didn't want you any more, he wasted no time in getting to the point, no time beating around the bush—just scheduled a transfer and breezed out of your life.

'How are you feeling?' Molly smiled down at the girl, noticing her red eyes and pinched face. 'Not too good, huh?'

'I'm just…' Bernadette gave a frustrated shrug '…fed up.'

'I don't blame you.'

'Stupid leg….' Bernadette sniffed. 'It's never going to get better.'

'It will,' Molly said. 'It's just taking a long time.'

'What's idio—idiom—?'

'Idiopathic?' Molly said, and Bernadette nodded.

'I heard the doctor saying it to my mum. What does it mean? Have I got cancer?'

'No, you don't,' Molly said firmly, wishing that grown-ups would think about little ears before they bandied big words about. 'It's nothing to be scared of. Idiopathic means "no known cause". Osteomyelitis can be caused by injury or trauma, or by an infection that spreads—only in your case they haven't been able to pinpoint any reason or find out why it happened.'

'And that's all that it means?' Bernadette checked.

'That's it.' Molly nodded.

'Well, I hate idiopathic…' Bernadette kicked her good leg in frustration and Molly knew exactly what she meant.

Knew because she hated the word too.

Hated it that there was no reason the doctors could find that she couldn't have babies—hated it that there was nothing wrong, which meant there was nothing that could be fixed.

'Is there anything else worrying you, Bernadette?'

'No.' Bernadette took a breath and for a second Molly thought she was about to tell her whatever else it was that was troubling her, but Bernadette changed her mind and shook her head. 'It doesn't matter.'

'It does to me.'

'You wouldn't understand.' Bernadette turned her face away, crossed her arms over her chest and promptly set off the IV alarm. 'I don't want to talk about it.'

'You're getting all tangled,' Molly said, straightening out the tubes and resetting the IVAC. 'We've got a new patient coming in—a six-year-old with a head injury. I've put her next to you.' Normally Bernadette would have a million and one questions—what had happened, what was her name, did Molly need her to look out for the new patient, to press the bell? Only not tonight. Tonight Bernadette just shrugged one tight shoulder and carried on staring at the wall.

'Even if I might not understand,' Molly said to the back of Bernadette's head, 'if you decide that you do want to talk about it, press the bell.'

'Talking's not going to help.' Bernadette sniffed. 'It doesn't change things.'

'I don't agree. Sometimes talking to your friends can change things.'

'You're just a nurse, though.'

'I'm your friend while you're here,' Molly offered. 'If you want me to be. Mind you, I should warn you that I'm not very good at sharing, and I'm not really in with the in crowd…' Pleased to see a near smile on Bernadette's pale lips, Molly chose not to push it. 'Up to you.'

'So you used to work here?' Anne Marie had made coffee, opened a packet of chocolate biscuits and was interrogating Luke by the time Molly finished her round and sat down. 'How long ago?'

'Five years.' Luke didn't look up from the notes he was writing, but he did take a biscuit or three. 'Then I moved to Sydney.'

'Why?'

'My wife's family lives there.'

'Oh!' Deflated, Anne Marie looked as if she was about to snatch back the biscuit he was holding as Molly gave frantic eye signals to tell her to stop. 'So you're married?'

'Widowed.'

'Oh!' It was a very different 'oh' this time as she pushed the whole biscuit packet in his direction. 'Do you have children?'

'Twins!' Luke said abruptly. 'Angus and Amelia— they're four.'

'How?' Anne Marie asked, as only Anne Marie could. 'What happened?'

'She was run over.' His lips were tight, his face grim as he wrote, but Molly knew that if he hadn't wanted to answer then he wouldn't have, knew that he was probably grateful in some way for Anne Marie's rather oddball directness, that he probably just wanted to get it over with. 'It happened six months ago. She was a doctor here too.' He looked up from the notes and to Anne Marie, 'You might remember her. Amanda Metcalfe.'

'Anne Marie's only been here a couple of years,' Molly said quickly.

'I arrived just in time for all this madam's dramas!'

'Dramas?' Grateful for the change of subject, Luke actually smiled. 'Oh, your divorce.'

'It's nothing to grin about!' Molly scolded, but she was smiling too.

'What a sad lot we are…' Anne Marie dunked her biscuit in her coffee.

'You too, then?' Luke asked, because—well, Anne Marie was waiting for him to! 'What's your tale of woe?'

'I haven't got one.' Anne Marie pouted, standing up as a patient bell went. 'Dead boring, me!'

'I don't think so somehow.' Luke grinned as she wandered off. 'Is she always that direct?'

'Always.'

'Well, at least it saves me from telling everyone. I'm sure Anne Marie will take care of that for me.'

'She won't—believe it or not, she's actually really discreet. She is,' Molly insisted as he gave a rather disbelieving frown. 'So, how does it feel to be back?'

'Weird!' Luke said. 'Familiar but different. Hard to explain, I guess.'

He'd done a very good job. It was so, so familiar, sitting at the nurses' station, gossiping, smiling. It unsettled Molly how easily they'd slipped back into ways of old, chatting easily, sort of friends again, yet it was so, so different.

Sipping her coffee, every now and then she looked over to where he was working, his blond hair falling forward as he wrote his notes.

Five years ago she'd loved him.

Absolutely, with all her heart loved him.

Had longed to get to work in the morning just to see him.

Had held her breath when she'd heard he'd broken up with the gorgeous Amanda.

Had almost fainted when he'd asked her out.

Had then longed to finish work just to be alone with him.

'Hey, I was just thinking…' He looked up, with green eyes that had once adored her, and Molly burnt the roof of her mouth taking too big a gulp of her coffee. 'Do you want to get breakfast after work in the canteen? We've got a bit of catching up to do.'

There was no right answer, Molly realised as she replaced her mug on the bench. If she said no, then he'd know how much he'd hurt her, might guess that as of three hours ago she'd realised that she wasn't actually over him. But if she said yes—well, sitting across the table from him, just the two of them, he was probably going to work it out anyway!

'I can't,' Molly settled for instead, grateful that she actually had an excuse. 'I'm meeting Richard for breakfast tomorrow.'

'Richard?'

'My ex,' Molly explained.

'That's very civil.'

'We are,' Molly said, squealing inwardly in delight at how well she'd handled that one. OK, she wasn't thin and in her cocktail dress, but *somehow*, for the first time in her entire life, she'd managed to play it cool!

'Another time, then,' Luke said.

'Sure.' Brimming with new-found confidence, she even managed a smile as she casually stood up and slowly walked off, only letting out her breath and breaking into a burning blush when she finally made it the restroom.

Contained—the elusive word she'd been looking for to describe Luke popped into her head.

He looked more contained than the laughing, care-free doctor she'd fallen head over heels in love with.

Tireder, sadder, older…a little more contained. And why wouldn't he be, given all that had happened? Molly thought, staring into the mirror at her own reflection. With a jolt she recognised that the sparkle that had been absent for so long was back in her eyes, her heart was fluttering that little dance that it hadn't for the longest time, and she had a slight smile on her full mouth and that lovely, euphoric feeling that came when you either drank champagne or…

Oh, no!

She really didn't have time for this.

Didn't have time to be flirting and blushing and wondering where, how, or if it was going anywhere. And she really, really wasn't ready for this.

CHAPTER TWO

'OFF for your breakfast?' He was walking along the corridor beside her.

'I've got to drop the car at the mechanic first for its service. Yes, then breakfast. What about you?'

'Race home, get the twins dressed and then take them to kindergarten, then bed.'

'So what are they like?' Molly asked because she was interested. 'The twins.'

'Different as chalk and cheese.' Luke grinned. 'Angus is practical, serious. Oh, he has fun and everything, but he's just straight down the line…'

'And Amelia?'

'Dramatic!' Luke rolled his eyes. 'A right little minx, actually. She's got me completely wrapped around her little finger—and she knows it.'

'Sounds like fun.'

'Not lately.'

And they stopped.

Stopped in a corridor, and for the first time really looked at each other.

'I'm sorry.'

'We're not saying that—remember?'

'Even so.' She couldn't look at him now and scuffed the floor with one of her feet. 'I know it's hard sometimes, hard pretending that you're OK…'

'It is,' Luke agreed.

'*Telling* everyone that you're OK,' Molly ventured.

'Just because they want to hear it,' Luke finished.

And even if they weren't, as they started walking Molly felt as if they were holding hands.

Holding hands through turbulent times.

Not that she'd been alone.

Friends had rallied round and family had gathered when Richard had walked out, walking out on them. On her.

There had been life rafts aplenty as she'd drifted for a while.

And, yes, they'd steered her to a place that was calmer— a place that was safe, where she'd hidden for a while—only now came the hard bit.

And only the lost could understand.

Trying to survive on an island that was empty.

Trying to keep warm with a fire that kept going out.

And trying to fathom if you could ever risk the journey again.

'I miss the casseroles.' Luke nudged her into a smile as they walked on. 'The mums at kinder set up this roster.'

'I miss the cakes.' Molly smiled. 'And the take-aways. I don't think I cooked for a month!'

'So do you two do that often, then?' They were stepping out into the ambulance bay, blinking as if they'd just come out of the movies at the bright morning sun— both talking fast, both on that slightly euphoric high that came at the end of a night shift when you should be tired, but you're not. 'Richard and you, do you meet up often?'

'No…' Molly thought about it for a moment. 'Just when we've got something to discuss, but that's getting less and less often now.'

'It's good that you can still be friends.'

'Oh, I wouldn't call it that.' Molly grimaced. 'To tell you the truth, I'm not looking forward to it all.'

'Text him, then,' Luke half joked and half dared. 'Give him some lame excuse and come and have breakfast with me instead.'

'Why would I even bother to text him?' Molly joked back, but she was walking to her car. 'Surely if there's one person you can stand up without guilt or lame excuses, it's your ex.'

'Well?'

They were at her car and she was surprisingly tempted to do just that. Funny…a night of gentle flirting with Luke and she'd forgotten to be nervous about meeting Richard, but she was wanting to get there now, wondering what it was that he wanted to discuss and sort of knowing what it was too.

Torn between convincing herself she was just being paranoid and bracing herself to face up to the truth.

'I'd better go.' There was more than a hint of regret in her voice. Luke this morning was an infinitely preferable option to hearing whatever it was Richard wanted to *discuss*. Luke's green eyes were tired but smiling, and he needed a good shave, and he looked like he'd looked in the mornings. Apart from the clothes and the packed car park, she could almost imagine his face on the pillow beside her.

'Ooh, is that the time?' Molly pretended to look at her watch. 'I'd better get a move on.'

'You know, it's actually nice, being back.' Luke smiled down at her. 'And it's been really nice to see you. I wasn't sure how you'd be, after what happened and everything.'

'It was a long time ago,' Molly pointed out, 'and given all that's happened to you, well…'

'I don't need your sympathy, Molly.' He said tightly. 'It's just good that we seem friends again—which we were. I mean, we were good friends…before.'

Before.

One little word that didn't quite match the passion and the pain it stood for—but it was far safer and far easier to relegate it to that. Far easier to just call it *before* than to actually discuss it.

'It's good to have you back,' Molly agreed. 'And you're right—it's good that we're friends.'

'Thanks for coming.'

'No problem!' Molly lied, slipping into the chair opposite Richard. 'It's good to see you.'

There were a million and one self-help books and Molly had surely read them all, but not one of them could actually do it for you.

Not one of them could actually tell you how to walk into a café and face your ex, whether you should kiss him on the cheek, or not, shake hands, or…just do as Molly did and pick up the menu and pretend to read it.

Not one of them could actually be there for you when,

despite appearances, despite the bright smile, despite the brave face, Molly knew this was going to be another of the blackest days of her life.

'There was something you wanted to tell me?' Ordering her latte, Molly scanned the menu, trying to decide whether to get honey on muffins, or the cinnamon toast, perhaps, which was always nice.

'It's a bit awkward.' Richard took a deep breath as Molly read on.

'I might get the scrambled eggs. Ooh, or maybe mushrooms on toast.'

'You see, I didn't want you to hear from anyone else. I thought it was right that I be the one to tell you—'

'I might just go the whole hog and get—the full breakfast, please.' She beamed at the waitress. She'd sworn she'd be cool for this moment, had prayed, had pleaded to any god that might be listening that she'd somehow manage a smile and congratulations when she heard that Jessica was pregnant, but she couldn't do it, couldn't sit there and smile, so instead she cried, just promptly burst into loud tears as Richard peeled off napkins and handed them to her. It made her feel worse, not better, that he was blowing his nose too, that his eyes were glassy and he was taking her hands and holding them.

'I'm so sorry, Molly.'

'Don't say that!' she sobbed. 'Because you shouldn't be sorry, you should be happy. This is good news. It's good news!' she said again, because it was. Richard always wanted to be a dad, would make a wonderful father. He shouldn't have to be apologising for something wonderful.

'I know.'

'And I'll be fine.'

'I know. I just know how much this must hurt.'

'You don't know,' Molly said, because he didn't any more. He'd joined the ranks of parents-to-be, just as, it seemed, everyone did in the end—everyone that was, but her. He'd seen her when she'd managed to smile at her sister's happy news, had held her hand when she'd visited friends in hospital, and had held her after, when she'd sobbed her heart out. Had held her and told her that one day, *one day*, they'd get there, be the parents they wanted so badly to be.

Well, now he had.

'I'm happy for you!' She managed a very watery smile. 'I know I don't look it, I know I'm probably embarrassing you…'

'You could never embarrass me.'

'But I really am very happy for you,' Molly gulped. 'You deserve this.'

And he did deserve it.

But, then, so did she.

The marriage hadn't ended because she hadn't been able to have a baby—over and over she'd told that to herself. Richard wasn't some bastard—as so many had made out—who had left her because she couldn't give him babies. They just hadn't been strong enough to survive the struggle, the endless, endless tests, the tears, the letdowns, the depression, the hell that was infertility.

He was a nice guy and she was a nice girl and they just hadn't made it.

'I'm actually not that hungry.'

'Don't go, Molly.' He was still holding her hand as she stood to go. 'I know—'

'No, Richard, you don't.' Molly shook her head and pulled back her hand. 'Please, don't make me sit here and reassure you that I'm OK. I will be OK. I just need to get through this bit—and I want to do it on my own.' And she turned to go, but changed her mind, turned around just in time to see a flash of relief on his face that this uncomfortable duty was over.

And for the first time she was angry.

Not that little bubble of anger that flitted in every now and then and was quickly quashed. Instead, this big pool of bile seemed to be being stirred up inside her, and she waited for a second, tried to swallow it down, but it just kept rising. She tried to reason with herself that by the time she walked back across the café to him it would have gone, that she would have calmed. She could see the nervous dart in his eyes as she marched back towards him and actually asked the question that had been churning for weeks in her mind.

'Is that why you filed for divorce?' She sat back down as Richard jumped to attention. 'I mean, you didn't waste a moment, did you? A year to the day exactly, the second you legally could, you filed the papers—you did. Are you getting married?'

'Jessica wants us to be married before the baby comes,' came Richard's logical answer. 'It's important to her.'

'But not very important to you.' She wasn't crying now, was sitting like a headmistress peering down her nose at a rather wayward child as the waitress brought her breakfast. 'Clearly, Richard, marriage isn't very important to you.' And if she hadn't embarrassed him before with her tears, she was doing a *much* better job now. A dull blush spread over his cheeks as her voice got louder and a couple of heads in the crowded café turned and looked. 'We can all *say* the right thing, we can all stand at the altar and *say* for better, for worse, in sickness and in health, we can all console ourselves that we're doing the right thing, and that we're being terribly civil and understanding by comforting our poor infertile ex-wife when the new tart's pregnant—but you know what? It's not about what we say, Richard, it's about what we *do*!'

'Then I tipped the whole lot, beans and everything, in his lap…' Molly sobbed on her mobile five minutes later to Anne Marie.

'Good for you!'

'And then I told him he could bloody well pay for breakfast!'

'Good for you.'

'I got really angry, Anne Marie. I mean really, *really* angry.'

'About time.'

Shutting the curtains on the bright morning sun, Molly bypassed the self-help books and turned off the phone. She grabbed a box of tissues, then climbed into bed. As her cat climbed up for a cuddle, Molly shrugged him off, then climbed out of bed and put him out of the room.

She didn't want to be some old spinster who kept cats, didn't want to feel so hollow and barren and less of a woman than she'd ever felt in her life

She *was* over Richard—despite having said it so many times. Like a big spear being pulled out of her side, Molly knew now that she finally was.

It wasn't Richard—it was her babies she was crying for this morning.

CHAPTER THREE

'MAYBE you could use a friend?' Bernadette was way too knowing for such tender years and at two a.m., when Molly was giving her her IV, two eyes had peeped open and said what no one else had dared. With Anne Marie on a night off, not one of the staff had commented on her very swollen, very puffy, heavily made-up eyes, and no one had mentioned Molly's impressive red nose and swollen lips—even Luke, apart from a small frown when he'd seen her, had had the decency to ignore them, but kids weren't so subtle.

'I'll be OK.' Molly smiled.

'I probably wouldn't understand anyway but, as you said, sometimes it's nice to have a friend.' Bernadette's eyes filled with tears, and Molly realised, with a sinking heart, that she finally wanted to talk, which was good and everything, just terribly bad timing.

'What's going on, honey?' Molly said.

'You won't laugh?'

'Not tonight,' Molly assured her.

'You'll probably say I'm too young…'

'I won't. Is it a boy?'

'I thought he liked me. And then Carly came and said

that they're going out, that they're going to the movies in a group, but she said that he's told her that he likes her—and she knew I liked him…'

'What's his name?'

'Marcus. I just hate being here, and I hate feeling like this.'

'Have you told your mum?'

'I told her I liked him ages ago, before I got sick, but she laughed and said I was too young for all that sort of thing. That I didn't *really* like him…'

'But you do,' Molly said simply.

'And I don't know what to do.'

'Cry?' Molly suggested, but really kindly, sitting on the bed and holding Bernadette's hand. 'Eat a lot of chocolate…that's what I do.'

'Does it help?'

'No!' Molly shook her head. 'Well, sort of—in the end you do feel better, but I don't know if that's the crying and chocolate or if you'd have felt better anyway.'

'I really do like him. I know I'm only twelve—'

'Hey, I fell in *love* at eleven!' Molly countered, and if she'd not been giving Bernadette her full attention she might have heard Luke come in to the room, might have seen two shoes appear beneath the curtains, would have caught his eye as he poked his head around and told him without words that unless it was urgent she'd be there in a few minutes. But instead she carried on talking. 'His name was Darren and he was gorgeous. He had big hazel eyes with really long eyelashes and sort of slightly buck teeth, but they suited him. Anyway, my friend Leslie said he was awful. He asked me if I was coming ice-skating on the weekend and I said I had to check with my mum. Well, I had to go to a christening and on the Monday I found out that Leslie had gone ice-skating and the next thing I knew…'

'Were you really upset?'

'I cried for a month,' Molly said. 'In fact, I could cry right now, this very minute, when I think about it. He was lovely. He still is.'

'You know him now?'

'Vaguely.' Molly shrugged. 'He's married to Leslie and they have a farm, so it worked out well, really—I don't think I'd be a very good farmer's wife.'

'Why?'

'I'd forget to set the alarm clock in the morning or something—and the cows wouldn't get milked and would probably end up with mastitis. I'm not very good with animals.'

'So it was probably for the best.'

'Probably.' Molly nodded. 'Only it didn't seem that way at the time.'

'So you really have felt like this! But it gets better, doesn't it?'

'Duh!' Molly pointed to her swollen eyes. 'Hey, Bernadette, strap on your seat belt because you're in for a bumpy, horrible ride, but it's fun too and exciting at times—wonderful, in fact.'

'It doesn't feel wonderful.'

'It will.' Molly smiled. 'And then it will be awful again for a while and you'll swear off men for life, then the next thing you know…' She gave a little shrug. 'I'm probably saying all the wrong things and scaring the life out of you.'

'It's nice to talk, though,' Bernadette sniffed. 'I actually do feel a bit better!'

'Friends do that for you,' Molly said, and stood up. 'Cry, eat chocolate and talk to your friends—but choose them carefully.'

'Carefully?' Bernadette frowned.

'You'll work it out.'

'Oh, you mean…'

'The Carlys and Leslies of the world!' Molly nodded. 'I'd better go. I've got a baby to feed. I'll talk to you later.'

Oscar Phillips was one of those gorgeous chunky babies who just lived to be fed, grabbing at his bottle with two fat hands, his mouth and eyes wide open before Molly had even sat down at the nurses' station.

'Don't worry, Oscar, food's coming,' Molly assured the baby, glad when Luke came past and picked up the phone, which was ringing.

'Hello, Mrs Phillips. He's being fed at this moment!' Luke grinned down the phone. 'He seems fine. I'll just check with the nurse who's looking after him.

'It's Oscar's mum, just checking in,' Luke mouthed to Molly.

'He's been good.' Molly nodded as Luke relayed the message and chatted with Oscar's mother for a moment or two.

'Thanks for that.' Molly sent a weary smile to Luke.

'Anything else I can do for you?'

'Nope.' Molly shook her head. 'You might even get some sleep.'

'No chance. I've got a couple of kids down in Emergency

that need admitting and I want to go and check in on Declan over on ICU.'

'How's he doing?'

'Better,' Luke replied. 'I think they might send him back to the ward tomorrow. I'll pop up later.' He turned to go, then changed his mind. 'And, by the way, I think you'd have made a lovely farmer's wife.'

'Luke!' She was genuinely appalled. 'Were you listening? That was private!'

'I couldn't help myself.' He laughed. 'I came to see if you had anything else for me to do—then I heard you talking and realised I probably shouldn't disturb you. And then...' He stopped laughing and looked at her, and she could feel his eyes taking in every bit of make-up and somehow taking in with it every bit of her brave face. 'I think you'd be a wonderful farmer's wife and even if you're not very good with animals, you're wonderful with children. You did a great job in there.'

'Poor little thing.' Molly smiled in the vague direction of Bernadette's room.

'And what you said was right,' Luke said gently. 'It really is good to talk to friends.'

'I know,' Molly said. She knew what he was offering only she couldn't take it. 'But not just yet.'

'How about breakfast?'

'I really *don't* want to talk about it.'

'Then don't,' Luke said. 'We can sit in silence if you want. I'll meet you in the canteen after your shift. No excuses.' His pager shrilled, making little Oscar's eyes, which were starting to close, pop open. Luke gave a wry smile as he pulled it out of his pocket. 'Except this one!'

Declan behaved, Emergency behaved, even Luke's pager behaved, which meant that twenty three hours, practically to the minute, since she'd had breakfast with Richard, Molly sat with a coffee, in a room full of people, with a man she'd once loved, and tried, once again to be brave.

'I'm not going to talk about it.' She stabbed at the plate of bacon, eggs, sausages and mushrooms he'd plonked in front of her.

'Fine,' Luke said, attacking his own breakfast. 'There's no brown sauce.'

'There never is. Here…' Molly pulled a few sachets out of her apron pocket. 'I nicked some from the ward. Actually, if you knew what happened yesterday, you might have thought twice about buying me a cooked breakfast.'

He didn't say anything, was busy buttering his toast and then ladling the entire contents of his plate, beans and all, into a vast sandwich, which was what he'd always done, Molly remembered. Unlike her, who left her toast to the very end and used it to mop her plate.

'I threw the lot in his lap.' She watched him smile with a very full mouth. 'You probably think I'm awful now.'

Luke swallowed. 'Did he deserve it?' he asked.

'I'm not sure—but I thought he did at the time.'

'Then I don't think you're awful.' He stared at her plate, and her hands, and there was just a tiny flicker of nervousness in his eyes. 'Eat up, Molly.' He grinned. 'There's a good girl.'

'Oh, you don't have to worry! Not that you didn't deserve a greasy lapful at the time, but I'm over you now.'

'Good.'

She gave him a slightly wicked smile. 'And, lucky for you, I'm starving.'

'Well, that's a relief.'

'And we're friends now,' Molly said.

'We are,' Luke confirmed. 'And that's good too.'

'Jessica's pregnant.'

'Jessica?' Luke said carefully.

'Richard's girlfriend. And I'm happy for him, I really am. I mean, I don't even want children, which was the problem in the first place. He wanted babies and I wanted my career.' If she said it enough, one day she'd actually believe it. Anne Marie had told Molly she was mad, of course, that she should lean on more people, let everyone know what she'd been through, was still going through. Only Molly couldn't—couldn't stand the sympathetic looks, preferred people to think it was by choice that she was childless.

'I never realised you were so career-minded!' Luke voiced his surprise. 'You were a great nurse, of course. I just always thought that…'

'What?'

'It just seems a strange choice of career—I mean, to work with children if you don't actually like them.'

'I do like children.' Molly gave a tight smile. 'And then I like being able to come home. Anyway, it doesn't make sense. I mean, if I worked on the oncology ward, it doesn't mean I want cancer.' It was a line she'd used more than a few times, and after a moment's thought Luke gave an accepting shrug and a nod.

'Good point.'

'It was just a bit of a shock, I suppose…' she gave another tight smile '…that he was having a baby. Anyway, it doesn't matter. I'm fine with it now. I'd really rather not talk about it.' She barely paused for breath. 'You see, I think I was so surprised because I thought Jessica was his transition girl.'

'Transition girl? I'm not with you.' Luke frowned, smothering his smile with a forkful of bacon as Molly had just refused to talk about it!

'You know—it's in all the books: after you come out of a relationship, you have your transition person— someone who's just there to help you get over what's happened, to massage your ego, sort of an evolution thing, to help you move on. You both know it's not going anywhere, it's not supposed to be *the one*. And I just assumed that that was what Jessica was.'

'His transition girl?' Luke frowned.

'Yep. Only it turns out she wasn't. They're getting married. Sorry.' Molly was embarrassed all of a sudden. 'I know I go on sometimes.'

'It's good to talk.'

'It is,' Molly agreed, then took a deep breath, forced herself to look at him as she forgot about herself. 'Do you?'

There was a horrible silence, a wave of pain surging towards her as his face creased and he visibly struggled to speak. When he did, he said two words she'd never heard from him.

'I can't.'

Because Luke always *could*, always had a solution to everything—even if meant calling in the boss. There was nothing Luke couldn't do. Except this. Molly felt tears fill her eyes again, only they were for him. Her hands held his and she didn't care if anyone was watching or looking because this wasn't about them, it was about him.

'I can hardly stand to think about it, let alone talk about it.' His eyes screwed closed as he held it all in. 'I just keep on keeping on, for the kids.'

'If you ever do,' Molly offered, 'want to talk about it…'

'I know.' Luke nodded, taking back his hands, even managing a half-smile. He was a little embarrassed, Molly guessed, that she'd glimpsed his pain, and quickly changed the subject. 'So, er, have you had your transition guy?'

'Heavens, no.' Molly mopped up the last of the egg on her empty plate with her toast. 'It's way too soon. Have you?'

'Oooh, there's a question!' He scratched at his chin for rather a long moment and the conversation that had flowed so easily just, *just* tipped into inappropriate—and perhaps that line of topic wasn't the most sensible one to follow, Molly realised, as they both rather awkwardly stood to go and then walked along the corridors and out into the ambulance bay. They stood horribly uncomfortably, facing each other. Perhaps it hadn't been the most sensible conversation to have with your ex.

Who you still really fancied.

Especially when you were a bit woozy from a day of crying and a long, long night shift.

'Where are you parked?'

'At the mechanic's!' Molly answered. 'It took me so long to get to sleep that by the time I woke up…'

'Do you want a lift?'

'I'll get the tram,' Molly said firmly.

'It's really no problem.'

'Don't you have to get home for the twins?'

'They've got kindergarten today—Mum stayed over last night and she's taking them.' He'd pulled out his car keys, was sort of jangling them between his fingers, and if they were just friends, she should just say yes, Molly thought, jump in the car and yawn her head off all the way home. Only they couldn't be just friends, Molly realised, because her heart was hammering in a way it didn't when Anne Marie offered her a lift, and eye contact was suddenly a terrible problem.

'I'll get the tram!' Molly said again, only this time to her shoes, telling herself she was being stupid, that there was no tension between them. Gosh, his wife had just died. As if he was even thinking…

'Molly…' His fingers lifted her chin, his delicious mouth a breath away as he said her name, and then it was on hers, and it felt so right, because it always had, so blissful, so familiar it actually hurt—hurt to taste again what she'd once devoured. She felt a sting of tears in her eyes as she kissed him back—a long slow kiss that neither wanted to end because then there would be questions that neither were really ready to answer. But end it did, and she still couldn't look at him, so she didn't, just buried her face in his chest as he held her for a moment.

'The staff car park's probably not the best place.' She tried a little joke, only it didn't work. 'I have to go.'

'I know.'

And she did have to go—had to walk away that very second without looking at him, had to put as much space as possible between them, before they both went and did something really stupid.

Really stupid, Luke said to himself as he started the car up and swiped his ID at the barrier. He could see her marching ahead, was tempted, so tempted, to wind down his window just to talk to her again. Feeling like a kerb-crawler as he did just that.

'You couldn't afford me.' Molly grinned, a little bit pink, her eyes a bit glassy, but she was smiling again, able to look him in the eye again, able to make him laugh as somehow she set the tone.

'Probably not.' Luke smiled back, and then his face became serious. He knew that a little kiss was big some-times—that it was probably her first kiss since Richard— and he didn't want to hurt her a fraction more than he already had. 'I actually wasn't about to whistle you in— I was just…' He didn't know how to voice it but, because it was Molly, he didn't really have to. 'You're OK?'

'I will be,' she answered, and because it was Molly she checked on him too. 'You?'

'Same!'

She probably thought he was feeling guilty, Luke realised as he drove off, glancing in the rearview mirror at the woman who consumed him. No doubt Molly thought six months was too soon to be over Amanda. He dragged his eyes back to the road, his face hardening as he indicated right and headed for home.

And for the hundredth, no, the thousandth, or perhaps even the millionth time, in the five years since he'd left her, Luke thought it again.

If only Molly knew.

CHAPTER FOUR

'TO OVERSLEEP once and leave your car at the mechanic's may be regarded as misfortune,' Anne Marie said loudly as they walked into work, and Molly could have hugged her as she fabulously misquoted, because it gave her a very good reason to be blushing as Luke looked up, 'but to oversleep twice can only be regarded as sheer laziness!'

'You overslept *again*?' Luke grinned.

'OK, OK,' Molly grumbled. 'I was exhausted. I just fell straight asleep and forgot to set my alarm.'

'Don't push it!' Anne Marie nudged her as they headed to the locker room. Because of course she hadn't fallen straight asleep—had spent the morning frantically reading her so-called 'help' books then angrily over-plucking her eyebrows while telling herself in the mirror that Luke was an utter bastard and she'd be completely mad to even *think* about getting involved with him again. And what a nerve he had to even think he *could* kiss her. How *could* she have let him?

'Don't leave me on my own with him.' Molly pulled on her stethoscope.

'Why—are you scared of him?' Anne Marie winked.

'Don't be stupid.'

'Scared you won't be able to keep your hands off him, more like! Don't worry, hen, I'll look after you! Anyway, we might be quiet—you might not even see him.'

'I wish.'

You really should be *very* careful what you wish for, Molly reflected as she gave handover the next morning, after an entire night without so much of a glimpse of Luke. Out of twenty-two sick kids not even one of them had managed a raised temperature, not one lousy IV chart or prescription to write up and the two empty beds that, despite a full to bursting emergency department, had remained empty. Even on the two occasions he'd rung to check if he was needed, Debbie or Anne Marie had answered the phone.

How was she supposed to play it cool, Molly huffed, when he wasn't around?

'Rita wants to do my appraisal while the ward's quiet.' Anne Marie rolled her eyes as Molly came out of handover. 'Do you want to go to the canteen and grab a coffee?'

'I'll just get the tram.' Molly yawned, pulling out her hair-tie. 'And I'll remember to set my alarm this time.'

Actually, she'd key a reminder into her mobile, Molly decided, blinking as she stepped out into the bright morning sun, tapping away.

'Oy, have you been avoiding me?' Luke made her jump as he caught up with her and made her smile too. 'What a night! It was steaming in Emergency.'

'I wish we'd been busy.' Molly yawned again, because now she'd started she couldn't stop. 'You know, I'm more tired when I'm doing nothing.'

'Stop it!' Luke scolded, also yawning. 'Now look what

you've done.' He gave her a very nice smile, but Molly couldn't help but notice he didn't offer her a lift. 'See you, then.'

'See you.' Molly smiled.

'Sleep well!'

'I will.' Molly nodded, wishing her legs would move and wishing his would too, but still they stood there. 'You sleep well too.'

'I will.'

'Right—see you then.' She was really going this time—well, she would have, Molly decided if he hadn't *then*, very casually offered her a lift.

'Sure.' Molly shrugged. 'But only if it's not out of your way.'

'Not at all.' Luke also shrugged. Only it was—miles and miles out of his way, as it turned out, because of course even if she hadn't completely moved on in other ways, she'd moved house several times since they'd last been together.

'Left here…' Molly sneaked a surreptitious look as she gave directions. She didn't usually like blond men, only he was so tall and so big and so…just so Luke. Actually, he could have come in orange with green stripes and he'd still have made her toes curl. 'And then a quick right at the roundabout.'

His mind clearly wasn't on the road, because he missed the quick right and they had to go round the roundabout again—Molly rigid and leaning back, trying not to lean into him, moving her hands quickly when he moved his to change gear, even frowning at the dashboard, because according to that he had climate control on…only she was roasting.

Maybe his climate control wasn't working, Molly thought helplessly as her house loomed into view. Well, obviously it wasn't working, because Luke was turning up the fan at that very moment, blasting them both with a shock of cold air that surely hissed into steam the second it hit their cheeks.

'Here!' Molly croaked. 'I'm the house before the white car.'

'Right!' Luke nodded, missing it by a mile and having to execute a hasty U-turn. 'Is this the one?'

'That's the one.' Molly beamed, scrabbling in her bags for her keys. 'Thanks ever so much for the lift.'

'My pleasure.' Which made him sound like he was giving a political speech! 'So you live here?'

'I do!' Molly's smile was rigid. 'Er, do you fancy a quick one?' Her face went from red to purple as Luke gave her a rather startled look. 'A quick coffee or something—before you drive home, I mean.'

And he lost a zillion brownie points at that point.

The million-dollar lottery dropped to a few cents as he faltered with indecision.

They'd driven fifteen kilometres, for goodness' sake. *Surely* he should have worked out his answer to the inevitable question before they got there. *Surely* he should be the one dealing with this—should have smiled and said no, or should have already turned off the engine before they headed inside.

'Whatever.' Molly beamed to his rigid profile. 'I guess I'll see you at work tonight…'

She never got to finish, never even got her keys out of her bag. A wedge of muscle was suddenly pinning her against the car seat, a mouth was knocking the breath out of her. Had there been any breath, Molly thought faintly as his tongue reacquainted itself with hers—because she'd stopped breathing at the roundabout. But, God, it felt good, he felt good, they felt good. The lottery payout ding-a-ding-dinged as it rose—a sort of battle with arms and legs and confined space, and neighbours putting their bins out and a dog barking.

'Coffee?' Molly croaked again, pulling back as she completely gave in.

'Sounds marvellous!'

Keys really were the most ridiculous, unevolved things. It was the twenty-first century, for goodness' sake, Molly thought as she smiled and waved at her neighbour and tried to get the sliver of metal into the smallest of slots— tried to stop the cat as he shot for freedom, tried to just make it through the front door.

'Coffee?' She turned as they entered, said it yet again, with conviction. There was for a while a sliver of hope that they might make it to the kettle—but Luke didn't even deign to answer. Just grabbed her and kissed her all the way to the bedroom.

And what a mess it was!

Littered with self-help books, a magnifying mirror and tweezers on her bedside table and—of all the *awful* things to have on display—her bed was awash with tissues, tiny sodden balls that screamed of pain. But he dusted them away with one hand, cleared the mattress in almost one stroke, before an angry cat almost took his hand off.

'Hell!' Luke cursed, sucking on the scratch as for the

second time in a couple of days the cat was deposited out of the bedroom, but for such a nice reason this time.

'I'm supposed to be playing it cool,' Molly whimpered as he grabbed her again.

'You're not cool, though,' Luke breathed. 'You never were,' he added between kisses. 'Don't ever change.'

And whoever said you shouldn't go back to your past was wrong, Molly decided as she frantically stripped off his clothes and he did the same to her. Whoever said that sex for sex's sake ultimately didn't satisfy had never had a six-foot-three Luke Williams raring to go in their line of vision. Whoever said that ultimately she'd regret it might just well be right, Molly accepted as he kissed away her pain, as his tongue slid over her body and washed away the years—but she'd deal with that later. And, yes, her bottom and boobs were just a little bit bigger than when last they'd met, but Luke didn't seem to mind a jot.

'Oh, Molly, I missed you!'

He wasn't supposed to say that, Molly thought help-lessly. This wasn't supposed to be about looking back or looking forward. This was supposed to be all about now.

'I missed you too,' Molly admitted, even if she shouldn't.

Oh, but she had.

Missed his sexy body, missed how he made her laugh, missed, missed, *missed* that he could be so into her, ravish-ing her, tasting her, grabbing handfuls of flesh as if he needed it to survive.

'I want you so much…' He just groaned it out. They were kneeling on the bed, grabbing at each other, kissing each other, revelling in each other. And then he just gathered her towards him, and the theory was it was way too quick and way too soon, but it was exactly how she was feeling.

'I want you too,' she whimpered, just holding him in her hand, guiding him into her, leaning on him, wrapping herself around him, lost in her own feelings but utterly safe and sound, awash with her own orgasm but drowning in his, feeling him within her and somehow knowing that what was happening was big.

Very big.

And very scary, because according to Luke she was still hung up on Richard, and according to Molly he was still grieving for Amanda.

Her head was on his chest, his blond chest hair on her cheeks, his arm holding her, and she could only guess at the expression on his face. She could feel the pensiveness in the moment, and wondered not just what he was thinking but who he was thinking about. But she was too scared to look and not ready to ask.

'Don't ignore me at work tonight.' Wriggling out of his embrace, she turned on her side, stared up at her bedside table, tried and failed to fathom that Luke was here in bed beside her.

'Why would I ignore you?' He was making tiny circles with his fingers in the small of her back.

She ignored his question and carried on speaking. 'Because you might regret it.'

'Not for a second.'

'I might,' Molly said.

'Ignore me or regret it?'

'Both…' She was playing with one of her curls, pulling it out to its full length then letting it ping back, thinking out loud and trying hard to be honest. 'I just don't want to get involved.'

'Er, at the risk of stating the obvious—' Luke started.

'I mean,' Molly broke in, absolutely aware they were lying in bed, absolutely aware they had just had sex and no doubt they would again, but possibly more scared than she'd ever been in her life. Because losing Luke, losing Richard, *that* she could deal with, *that* she had dealt with, only staring over at him, staring into those jade eyes, feeling him all big and strong and male beside her, feeling the peace his body brought hers, it was her mind she was scared for, because giving herself back to him, only to lose him again, would be too much to bear. 'What I'm trying to say is that I don't want to get involved like we were…' She swallowed hard, could hardly bring herself to go there in her mind, let alone say it. 'Before.'

'Molly, I know I hurt you. I know—'

'Don't.' She brushed his hand away. She could take affection, could take intimacy, even—she just wasn't ready for tender, lust-filled explanations. Just couldn't, wouldn't go there with him.

Because she already had.

She had given him her heart once and he hadn't treated it kindly, hadn't handled it with care, and she wasn't going to take that chance again.

CHAPTER FIVE

'HEY! Fancy seeing you here?' Luke had a point—midday in the admin corridor was the last place Molly would usually be. 'And looking very smart too!' He ran an approving eye over her chocolate-brown suit, and Molly shifted in her nipping high heels as he took in her bare, fake-tanned legs then dragged them back up to her for once carefully made-up eyes—slightly awkward eyes that couldn't meet his.

He'd rung her a couple of times since that morning, had tried to talk to her at work, but Molly either hadn't picked up or had been too busy.

And it wasn't about playing it cool this time—it was about playing it safe.

'I had an interview,' Molly mumbled. 'What about you?'

'Same.' Luke indicated his own very nice suit, 'Well, a first one anyway.'

'How did it go?'

'You never really know, do you? I can expect to hear from them shortly! How about you?'

'Same.' She could actually look at him now.

'So what was the interview for?'

'It's for a paediatric intensive care course—there are quite a few applicants, and most of them already work in Intensive Care, so I'm not that hopeful.'

'How long's the course?'

'A year—a pretty full-on year too. Still, it's something I really want to do—need to do,' Molly corrected herself, 'if I want to get on.'

'You are getting on.' Luke smiled. 'Fancy lunch?'

'No kids?'

'Mum's taking them to her sister's after kinder so I've got a couple of hours. Come on, we'll take my car and I'll drop you back here afterwards.'

Which was nice and easy.

So nice and easy that when they were sitting in a pub in their smart suits, tucking into steak sandwiches, Molly even managed to relax.

'We look like business people!'

'We do!' Luke grinned. And it was just something they did—or used to, Molly realised, people-watching or playing stupid little role-play games that didn't need the rules set out—because somehow they already knew them. 'Having a lunchtime meeting! What are we discussing?'

'My fantastic performance!' Molly winced at the opening she'd unwittingly given him.

'It was!' Luke winked. 'And the figure's certainly pleasing, and you're definitely easy to get along with…' He took a long drink. 'But…'

'There's always a but.' Molly sighed.

'I'm a bit concerned about your inability to commit— and communication hasn't been effective lately.'

'Ah-h, that!' He'd always been able to do that, Molly

remembered, always been able to get straight to the point and soften it somehow. Maybe there was a reason they liked their silly games, because it made those difficult things just a touch easier to say. 'Well, I'm not looking for anything permanent at the moment.'

'Molly.' He wasn't playing any more. He put down his drink and took her hands as she spoke to their fingers.

'I was very happy with the company,' Molly said, playing but not playing too. 'But not at the way my role was terminated. So…'

'I'm sorry for hurting you. Things were so, so-o…' He took one hand back, rubbed and then squeezed the bridge of his nose with his fingers, as if holding it in as he forced the words out. 'It wouldn't be like that again.'

'Because there's no Amanda to leave me for.' And there wasn't much he could say to that, so he didn't.

'So what happens now?'

'You drop me off, then pick up the twins, and I'll go and grab some sleep before work.'

'That wasn't what I was asking.'

'I know.' Molly gulped.

'Do you want to see me again?'

'Of course I do.' Molly's answer was so assured Luke was confused.

'But you said you didn't want to get involved.'

'I don't,' Molly said, and it took half a glass of lemonade before she was ready to explain further. 'I guess we just accept that we're not going to go anywhere. You know what we were talking about before—maybe we could be each other's transition person…'

'Oh, please,' Luke groaned.

'Why not? We've both been through a lot. A no-strings affair where we both just enjoy each other for as long as we….' she blew her fringe skywards '…enjoy each other, I guess.'

'Massage each other's egos?' Luke checked, and she nodded. 'Make each other feel good?'

'Sounds about right,' Molly said. 'And of course there'd be lots of fabulous sex!'

'Friends as well?'

'Absolutely.'

And in theory it sounded perfect, only Luke was gritting his teeth and sort of shaking his head. 'I don't know if I can do that. I mean, I don't know if that's enough for me. I really like you.'

'You were right before—you *really* did hurt me, Luke.' There, she'd said it, and because she'd said it once, it made it easier to say it again. 'You really hurt me—and I just don't know if I can get past that. I don't know that I could ever really trust you again—if I even want to try to trust you again. And then there's…' Her voice petered out and he took over.

'The twins?' he said, and she nodded. 'And that's not you?'

'It's not.'

'Could it ever be?'

'No,' Molly said honestly, because even if she wanted a baby, even if she wanted children, even if she'd met him for the first time today and he'd come with his own mini-football team, she could have accepted them. But they hadn't met today. They'd met five years ago—and she didn't want to raise Amanda's children.

Didn't want to raise the children of the woman he'd walked out on her for.

Didn't want to suddenly be good enough now that Amanda had gone.

And those were the rules—or her rules, at least—and for a little while he thought about it, his expression closed and unreadable until he leant across the table.

'Come here, transition girl.' He gave her a kiss, a very nice, very slow kiss that almost made her feel better—especially when he pulled back, especially when he looked into her eyes so deeply it burnt. 'We'll stay friends… whatever happens.'

'Of course we will.'

CHAPTER SIX

THREE short bursts on the patient buzzer had Molly locking the drug trolley and running.

'He's convulsing.' Louanna had pulled down the cot-side on the bed and had Bodey on his side, was turning on the oxygen at the wall as the little boy jerked and grunted. 'I was walking past and heard him.'

'He's burning.' Molly felt the hot little head as she held the oxygen mask over his rigid face. 'Fast-page Dr Williams!' Molly said as Anne Marie, alerted by the buzzer, ran in and grabbed the resus trolley. 'Louanna.' But she was already onto it, pulling the curtains around the other patients' beds so they couldn't see what was taking place. But though the four-bed ward was unusually empty, Molly caught a glimpse of Bernadette's pinched, worried face as again she was witness to just a bit too much.

Molly gave little Bodey rectal diazepam, which he had been written up for in an emergency. Debbie cool-sponged him, while the little body jerked beneath them. 'Where's Mum?'

The question was answered by Bodey's mother's

arrival, a moan of fear escaping her as she dropped her sponge bag.

'He's having another seizure,' Molly said calmly, as Debbie went over to her. 'He's going to be OK. He's got a temperature.'

A convulsion was a fairly routine emergency. Some babies and children were prone to them when they were febrile. But no matter how used the nurses were to dealing with them, they were still unpleasant and just awful for the mothers, and Debbie led Bodey's mother out to the corridor just as Luke arrived, breathless from running from Emergency.

'How long—?'

'Five minutes since we found him,' Molly answered, glancing up at the wall clock. 'He's had some rectal diazepam. I gave him some paracetamol five minutes before that.' The fitting was stopping now, the awful grunting and rigidness abating. Bodey dragged in big deep breaths and his rolled-back eyes started to shut. 'Bodey Andrews, five years old, admitted with a febrile convulsion following a query UTI,' Molly said. As night cover, it wasn't possible for Luke to know every patient and their history off the top of his head.

'Right…' Luke checked Bodey carefully, looking in his eyes, ears, his throat…flicking through the blood work that had been done in Emergency. 'Well, there's an infection somewhere. Have we got anything back on his urine yet?'

'I'll check on the computer, but nothing's come to the ward yet,' Molly said.

'What's he been like overnight?'

'He's slept. Afebrile at two, just woke up grizzly at half past five, so I gave him paracetamol.'

Bodey was starting to wake up now, scared and crying as Luke continued to examine him, pushing his head down onto his chest. 'Let's get some blood cultures now, while he's febrile.' Luke frowned in concern. 'Let's get him down to the treatment room—can you pull up his path results for me? And send his mum down. I'll talk to her there.'

'Is he okay?' Bernadette asked, once Bodey had been moved to the treatment room.

'He will be,' Molly said, 'though it must have been horrible for you to see.'

'I could hear him making all these noises, but I was asleep. I thought he was just snoring. Maybe I should have pressed the bell…'

'It's not your job to watch the patients!' Molly said firmly. 'And he did sound like he was snoring. These things just happen with little ones sometimes, when they get too hot. He's going to be OK.'

Only Luke wasn't so sure.

'He doesn't like the way he's holding his head, so he's going to do a lumbar puncture.' Anne Marie, now in a gown and mask, stuck her head around the door. 'And he's called Doug to come in.' Anne Marie's face was serious. 'You know we've had two with meningitis in the space of a week—remember the little one you specialled?'

How could she forget?

She had been called on her day off to see if she could do some overtime—specialling meant one-on-one nursing. In this case it had been for a child with a stent infection who had a complicated history of cerebral palsy and seizures—a child who had, it turned out, after Molly had spent a frantic night in a closed room with him, actually had bacterial meningitis and due to Molly's close contact with him she had had to be treated with antibiotic cover. 'I'm still on antibiotics.' Molly grimaced. 'But it happens like that sometimes. We don't even know if that's what's wrong yet!'

'I know,' Anne Marie sighed. 'Just my brain working overtime.'

It was just one of those really horrible mornings where nothing got done, and worse, Molly chewed over whether she had done enough for Bodey. He had been grizzly and febrile when he'd woken up, but had settled back to sleep, so much so that his mum had nipped out for a shower. And the dipstick on his urine had indicated a urinary tract infection, which would account for his temperature. All of this whirred through Molly's head as she gave out the drugs and ran errands for Anne Marie when she popped her head out of the treatment room more than a few times.

'We're moving him over to ICU.' It was Doug who stuck his head out this time. 'Could you ring and let them know we're leaving now?'

Which didn't go down too well. ICU had only just heard about the patient, but when Molly explained the consultant himself was bringing him over, there wasn't much they could say.

'Remind me again why I'm applying for a permanent job here?' Luke's face was grim as an hour later he raced back to catch up on his notes.

'How is he?'

'Seized again just as we got him over,' Luke said. 'Doug's with him now and so is the anaesthetist. I've got to write up some notes and hand over to Tom.'

'Emergency rang. They're sending up a patient in half an hour,' Louanna called out. 'Nathan Tomkins is thirteen years old. Where do you want him?'

'I told them not to send him till the day shift got here.' Molly ran an exasperated hand though her hair. They'd had two admissions from emergency at five a.m., then Bodey had had his convulsion and taken a bad turn, and with the day case theatre patients starting to arrive it had thrown the morning routine out of the window. And now this. 'I'll ring and tell them that they're going to have to wait. We're just too busy. And he's for traction, so the bed's going to take for ever to set up…'

Unfortunately, Molly never got to the phone. Emergency's version of half an hour differed from that of the rest of the world by about twenty-nine minutes. The ward doors opened and the new patient arrived, whether the children's ward was ready or not.

And it would serve no purpose getting angry in front of the patient, so Molly greeted Nathan warmly and told him they wouldn't be long, then, silently fuming, went to the storeroom, where Anne Marie was trying to scramble together the traction equipment.

'Thanks!' Molly let out an angry breath, then helped her colleague haul down the massive metal frame that would sit over Nathan's bed and the bracket that would support the weights. 'Imagine sending him at a quarter to seven in the morning.'

'ICU said exactly the same thing,' Anne Marie pointed out. 'But that's Emergency for you!' Anne Marie rolled her eyes. 'You know how busy they are, unlike the rest of the hospital.'

'Where shall we put him?' They were carrying the equipment between them, trying to come to rapid decisions that usually merited a bit more thought.

'In with the boys in room eight. Or he could go with Bernadette—she's sick of seeing people come and go, poor wee thing,' Anne Marie tutted. 'I was talking to Luke. He just got some blood back on her and he said that she's probably here for *another* fortnight at the very least. She could probably do with someone who's here for a while, but she's got her period, and I'm sure the last thing she wants is to share her room with a boy.' It was a juggling act that went on all the time in the children's ward—trying to balance teenagers with toddlers, boys with girls, long-stay patients with overnighters, and sometimes it was impossible, but they did try to get the mix as close to right as they could. Molly whizzed down to talk to Bernadette before she made her choice.

'I just thought it might be nice for you both to have some company around your own age—given that you're both going to be stuck here for a while. But if it's awkward for you with bedpans and all that...'

'No, no.' Bernadette was already sitting up in bed, waving to her new roommate through the glass window. Nathan was giving a sort of half-wave back. 'Bring him in.'

'You get on,' Anne Marie said to Molly, grinning at Bernadette's cheerful expression. 'Louanna and I will set up the traction and get him settled.'

Molly never really caught up after that. After giving handover, even though she was aching for bed, there were more than a few patient notes that needed to be updated before she could get there.

'Morning, Molly!' Tom, the resident, all nice and refreshed from a night in bed, grinned as he surveyed the chaos. 'You look exhausted.'

'Tell me about it!' Molly said, not even looking up from the notes she was writing.

'Actually, Luke, I was hoping to ask a favour…' Luke gave a grunt that sort of matched with Molly's mood as Tom went on. 'Any chance of you swapping so you work Saturday night for me? It's our wedding anniversary and I completely forgot and Shelly will never forgive me if I'm working—you know what it's like.' He halted suddenly. 'Sorry, Luke, I just didn't think.'

'It's fine.' Molly looked over as Luke gave a tight smile and managed a brief shrug. 'And it's fine about Saturday too. Actually, if you could do a weeknight for me, that would be great. Just makes things easier.'

Only it wasn't fine—in fact, it must hurt like hell, Molly realised, because not only was he juggling work and raising twins and doing everything that Amanda must have done, he was grieving for her too.

'Does it hurt all the time?' They were lying in bed, half awake and half asleep, and Molly could almost hear Luke's mind whirring.

Could feel the tension that, even after their lovemaking, hadn't left him this time.

'Not when I'm with you.' His face turned towards hers, jade eyes holding hers.

'Do you think about her all the time?' Molly asked, and watched his eyes become shuttered.

'Molly…' He gave an exasperated sigh. 'Where are we going with this?'

'I'm just trying to understand…'

'Well, you don't.' He sat up in the bed, dragged his hands through his hair. For a second she thought he was going to climb out, but instead he confronted her with a truth. 'You know, for someone who wants to keep things light, you're asking some pretty heavy questions.'

'I know.'

'I just don't want to go there, Molly.' He shook his head as she stared over at him. 'That's about Amanda and I…and it's not something I can share with someone who doesn't want to get too involved.'

This time he did get out of the bed, leaving Molly more confused than she'd ever been because, like it or not, deny it or not, getting involved was exactly what she was doing.

With her heart.

'What are you doing with these?' Luke came out of the bathroom, holding up a packet of antibiotics.

'They're rifampicin…' Molly blinked.

'I know what they are. I just didn't know you were on them.'

'That child who had bacterial meningitis…' Molly's throat was suddenly dry. 'Not Bodey—there was one last week when you were on nights off. I was specialling him before we knew what it was…' Her voice faded out, knowing exactly what he was thinking. She'd let him think she was on the Pill—and if she was on the pill then a week's course of rifampicin meant they should be taking extra precautions.

'And you didn't think to tell me!' Luke snapped. 'Or you just didn't stop and think. For heaven's sake, you're a nurse, Molly.' He was really angry now, pulling on his clothes. 'You want to be more careful, you know, because for someone who doesn't want to get involved, for someone who definitely doesn't want kids, you're walking on very shaky ground.'

Very shaky, Molly realised when later he rang to apologise, to check that she was OK, being nice and concerned, and just Luke.

'I wasn't the best anyway this morning.'

'Well, it wasn't exactly the best night to work.'

'You're telling me.' She could almost see his eye-roll. 'When I was taking the history his mum said something and it turned out that Bodey's little sister goes to the same kinder as the twins.' Luke sighed into the phone. 'I've just rung Doug and it would seem that Bodey's meningitis is more likely viral—the infection showing up in his blood work is actually from his UTI. But I left there this morning thinking there was a meningitis outbreak, wondering if I should send the twins to kinder today, just completely overreacting—you know what it's like.' He gave a soft laugh but it was aimed at himself. 'Oh, no, you don't, do you? You probably think I'm crazy.'

'Anne Marie was the same.' Molly's voice was unusually high.

'Kids...' Luke sighed. 'Who'd have them?'

And he hung up the phone with all the confidence and neurosis of someone who did.

Yes, very shaky, Molly realised, swallowing her antibiotic, telling herself that if he knew he wouldn't make such careless remarks, and telling herself that maybe it was time that he did...

CHAPTER SEVEN

'WHAT was she like?'

Doing their bit for the environment *and* their purses, since the mechanic debacle, Anne Marie and Molly had decided to take it in turns now and then to give each other lifts—but they were stuck in traffic, due to a crash on the freeway, and Anne Marie was asking questions as they crawled along at two kilometres an hour. Molly rather wished the emissions coming from her friend were from the exhaust pipe.

She'd been seeing Luke for a couple of weeks now, and because Anne Marie knew everything anyway, Molly had, of course, told her, making her cross her heart and hope to die that not only would she promise not to breathe a word but that she wouldn't interfere—which Anne Marie was extremely good at.

'Amanda—what was she like?'

'I never really got to know her.'

'But she worked with you.'

'Not much. She was from Sydney. She'd come to Melbourne for a paediatric rotation, but she only stayed for six months, and half the time she was on sick leave—

there was some family problem in Sydney she had to keep flying back for.'

'Still, you must have formed an opinion.'

'Superwoman!' Molly finally admitted.

'Tell me.' Anne Marie grinned at Molly's tense profile. 'What was Superwoman like?'

'Good-looking, funny…' Molly changed into second gear and the engine let out a groan of protest as they finally moved a couple of hundred metres. 'Thin, tall, blonde.' The car in front's brake lights weren't working, which made things even more difficult, and they jerked forward in their seats as Molly slammed on her brakes and ground the gears, along with her teeth. 'Intelligent, witty, sexy, organised…' Stalling in the middle of the freeway, Molly put on her handbrake and restarted the engine, praying the service on her ancient car had actually achieved something. It had—the car started again and the conversation resumed.

'Basically, she was everything I'm not.'

'So you hated her?' Anne Marie laughed.

'Sadly, no,' Molly sighed, nodding her thanks to the police officer who had waved her onto the hard shoulder and past the accident, 'though not for want of trying. She was also extremely friendly and nice— Oh, do you think we should offer help…?'

But nothing, not even a pile-up on the freeway, was going to stop Anne-Marie. She wound down her window and after a brief chat with the police officer, who said that everything was under control, turned her attention back to the—for Molly—painful subject.

'You were saying?'

'That we're going to be late,' Molly attempted, and Anne Marie didn't push, didn't say anything.

But maybe she *did* need to talk, maybe what had eaten her up for so long now really did need to be voiced.

'Luke and I were friends—really good friends. We just hit it off the day we met. I had a bit of a crush on him, well, any female with a pulse did, but he was already going out with Amanda when we met, and I knew I didn't stand a chance—it was nice to just be friends. Then suddenly they broke up. Out of the blue. I heard that they'd broken up and that she'd gone back to Sydney.'

'And?'

'We had a sick kid in one day—I know we have sick kids all the time but...' Molly's voice thickened for a moment at the memory. 'She died. I know it happens, I know we all deal with it, but we were both pretty upset. The next day was my day off, but that evening the phone rang—he'd got my number from the ward book and he rang to see if I was OK.' Molly frowned. 'We were friends at work, that was all, so ringing me at home was crossing the line. He asked if maybe I wanted to go out for a drink.'

'Which you did?'

'I was more than happy to cross the line.'

'You got on well?'

'Wonderfully well.' Molly sighed. 'We were only together for three months, but for the entire time, from the first date, we were inseparable. We were already friends and that just got better. It wasn't just sex, though that was great, and it wasn't just the romance. I can't really explain it...'

'Sounds a bit like love,' Anne Marie said, and Molly

sniffed loudly as she indicated to leave the freeway, because that was exactly how it had felt, at least to her. 'I was worried at first. I mean, I wanted to know that they'd actually split up, that she wasn't just in Sydney and they were taking a break, but, no, he told me they were washed up, that there was absolutely no chance of them getting back together. Then one Friday I was on a half-day and he rang and asked if we could meet. I thought it was strange. I mean we never actually formally *met*, it was either his place or mine, but we met in this café and he told me he'd made a mistake, that he was moving up to Sydney to be with Amanda and that it was over…' And even though she could tell Anne Marie almost everything, that bit she couldn't. Even five years on the words were too painful to repeat to herself, let alone someone else.

'Do you think she was pregnant? Do you think that's why he went back to her?'

'Probably—I don't know the twins' birthday, but I've done the maths and I guess she must have been.' The sign for the hospital blurred. Molly turned in, swiping her ID for the staff car park, and even though they were late as she pulled into her usual spot, neither woman made a move to get out. 'If he'd told me that, I could have understood. If he'd said that he had to make a go of things, I could have taken that.'

'Could you?'

'I think so.' Molly sniffed again. 'I mean, it would have hurt, but I would have respected why he was ending things. But, Anne Marie, what we had was good, so-o-o good. I utterly, utterly fell for him, held nothing back for myself, and never, not for a second, did I see it coming.

When he rang me, when I met him that day, it never even entered my head that he was about to end things. And it wasn't just that—it was *how* he ended it. It doesn't matter.'

'I think it does.'

'Not now…' Molly gave a grim smile. 'But if I've learnt anything from it, it's that I'll never trust him again.'

'Which isn't a very good basis for a relationship.'

'We're not in a relationship, though,' Molly pointed out.

'Come off it, Molly. You see each other all the time, you're sleeping together, you're both clearly crazy about each other—if that's not a relationship, then I don't know what is.'

'OK, maybe we are in a relationship of sorts, but I know this much—he'll never have that piece of me again.'

'What piece?' Anne Marie frowned.

'That piece you give of yourself. That piece of yourself that you normally don't let anyone else see, that piece of yourself that you trust the other person to take care of.' There was a wistful note to her voice as she recalled all they had shared, all they had once been, but her lips pursed with a bitter tinge of aftertaste, even after all these years.

'Be careful,' Anne Marie said, and Molly wished that she hadn't, wished Anne Marie would tell her she was being stupid, tell her, as she always usually did, to go for it, that it was time to live, time to get out and have some fun.

'Hey.' Molly tried to make light of it. 'Weren't you just saying the other week that I should get out there, start dating?'

'And move on from the past,' Anne Marie elaborated. 'And, yes, I know Luke's gorgeous, and I know he clearly likes you, it's just…well, he didn't treat you well.'

'I know.'

'And you deserve to be treated well.'

'I know that, too.'

'Just don't settle for anything even close to second best. Look, maybe I'm worrying about nothing.' She relented a touch. 'Maybe, with losing his wife, he's been through enough hell to come out a different man.'

It was scary how much Molly wanted to believe that he had, scary that, despite firm words, somewhere deep inside she was wavering, wanting to give him that piece of her she really ought to hold back—and wanting too that piece of Luke that, until she opened up, he wasn't prepared to give. 'Come on.' She heaved her bag from the car floor and opened the door. 'Or we'll be *really* late.'

'What's all the noise?' Molly asked sternly. 'I told you two to settle down half an hour ago.'

'Sorry!' Bernadette didn't look remotely sorry.

'Sorry...' Nathan mumbled. 'We were watching a movie...' He started laughing again and so too did Bernadette. Molly stood between their beds and looked up. They both had a television over their beds and had taken to wearing their headphones while watching the same show and shouting ever louder at each other.

'What are you two watching?' Molly asked, hoping that, given the lateness of the hour, she hadn't let them get away with watching something completely inappropriate. But it was one of her favourite comedies too, and Molly couldn't help but giggle herself as, even without headphones, she easily got the joke.

'Keep it down,' Molly warned as she left them to it.

'We've got a direct admission coming in.' Luke came into the kitchen to find her, where she was rummaging in the hospital fridge, trying to find some juice and sandwiches for one of her post-op patients who had woken up hungry. 'Carl Adams—an eight-year-old with asthma. That was his GP—he's seen the child several times over the past week and can't get it under control. He's coming in directly from the GP's to the ward. He's been in a few times.' He must have seen Molly's slight grimace. 'He'll be stuck down there for ever if I send him to A and E. There's been a big pile-up on the freeway and—'

'I know all that,' Molly agreed, 'but I'll be down a nurse for a while, because no doubt you'll want a chest X-ray.'

'No doubt!' Luke made no apology.

'I think I recognise the name,' Molly said. 'He was in a few weeks ago, actually. I'll ring Admissions and have his notes sent up.'

'I want a drink.' The spotty, moody face of Aaron Bowden peered round the door and made her jump.

'Please!' Luke stared over at his patient, who shouldn't be in the staff kitchen anyway.

'Please,' Aaron mumbled, taking the can of lemonade Molly offered. With Luke still staring, he offered a quick 'Thanks.' Then added, 'Oh, and my television isn't working.'

'I'll ring Maintenance in the morning.'

'But I was in the middle of watching a film!'

'It's eleven o'clock—you should be in bed,' Molly said, but Aaron just blinked at her and she gave in with a sigh. 'They're watching it in Room 2. Go and get your headphones. I'm sure they won't mind if you join them, but I'm telling you, and you can tell them, that if I have to come in about the noise again, all televisions are going off.'

'Thanks,' Aaron mumbled, without prompting this time. 'By the way…' His face was as red as his pimples as he turned to Luke. 'How was that kid—the one who had the fit the other morning?'

'Doing well.' Luke smiled. 'He should be back on the ward tomorrow.'

'Still big on manners, I see!' Molly grinned when Aaron had gone.

'Absolutely!' Luke nodded. 'Aaron's a nice kid under all that hair—he just comes across badly.'

'He's a teenager!'

'A teenager who's getting himself into all sorts of trouble,' Luke pointed out. 'I spoke to him last night. You know, I think he's really bright.'

'Aaron?' Molly frowned, wondering if they were talking about the same patient. 'He's failing in everything at school…'

'Because he's bored out of his skull, probably. I was taking some blood from him earlier and the news was on—they were talking about interest rate rises or something. I was only half listening, and he came out with a really smart comment. I nearly missed his vein. It was something really observant that you wouldn't expect a fifteen-year-old to say.' His eyes widened, along with Molly's. 'Especially Aaron. I'm going to see about getting him evaluated. I'll have to speak to his mum first *and*…' Luke grinned '…if I have unearthed a child genius, he's going to need a few manners when he goes for a scholarship interview.'

How could he have just given it all away? For the hundredth, maybe the thousandth time she asked herself. For some quick money? For convenient hours? Had he gone on to do the GP rotation she could have understood—his own patients, following them through, getting to know their families. All of that, Luke would have adored, but a walk-in, walk-out clinic just wasn't him. A script for antibiotics and a sick certificate for work for a nameless face wasn't the way Luke practised medicine.

Aaron Bowden was in for burns to his hands and neck—thanks to a stupid home experiment in the garden while he'd flunked school and his mother had been at work. The usual! But Luke had taken time with the young man. Had sat and chatted to him one night when a children's ward was the last place a teenager wanted to be, when it seemed every baby in the place was awake and all the toddlers were crying for their mums.

Luke had sat in the playroom with him.

Had turned down the chance for a precious couple of hours of sleep to play video games with Aaron and get to know him.

That was the sort of doctor Luke was—the sort of man he was.

And he was also a man who could reduce her to jelly with just a few choice words…

'Right…' He drained his glass. 'I just need to sign a chart for Anne Marie. Call me when the new admission gets here.'

'Please!' Molly called to his departing back, but he ignored her. 'Please!' she said more loudly, which, as Luke turned round, she realised had been his intention.

Her breath caught in her throat when he turned round and gave her *that* look—*that* look that told her and only her exactly what he was thinking—and topped it off with a tiny, knowing wink.

'Save the begging for later, Molly!' He grinned at her blush as he twisted her words deliciously. 'We're at work, remember?'

'What are you looking so flustered about?' Anne Marie asked when Molly came back to the nurses' station where a completely relaxed Luke was signing off the drug charts.

'I'm just hot,' Molly said, pointedly taking off her cardigan, then frowning when Luke came back onto the ward. 'And keep an eye on Room 2—there's a party going on.'

'They could use one!' Anne Marie said. 'And so could you!'

'Sorry?' Molly frowned.

'When was the last time you went to a party?' Anne Marie dunked her biscuit in her coffee as Molly pursed her lips. She knew what Anne Marie was up to, but she'd promised not to interfere, and she would have reminded her of that fact except Luke was standing there—Luke, who didn't actually know that Anne Marie knew. 'When was the last time you had a fabulous night out somewhere really nice?' Thankfully a call bell went and Anne Marie, as if butter wouldn't melt in her mouth, stood up. 'I'll get it.'

'That told me.' Luke gave a half-smile to her departing back. 'She's right.'

'She's meddling,' Molly said, 'which is what she does best. Is everything OK?'

'Everything's fine. I was just wondering…' He nodded his head towards the playroom '…if I could have a quick word.'

'Sure.' They never brought their relationship to work. Obviously Anne Marie knew, but apart from a quick flirt when they were alone, their *relationship* was strictly off the ward. Still, as Molly duly headed for the playroom, somehow she knew this wasn't about work.

'My mum's got an appointment at Outpatients this morning—at eight. It's at the Women's Hospital.'

'Is she OK?'

'She's having a few tests—nothing too serious, I think.' He gave a low laugh. 'And I'm not being evasive. It doesn't matter to her that I'm a doctor. As she keeps telling me, there are certain things she refuses to discuss with her son—whatever his profession.'

'Good for her.' Molly smiled, but there was a worried tinge to it. 'Are you concerned?'

'A bit,' Luke admitted. 'Still, if she doesn't want to talk to me about it, I'm not going to push it—for now, at least. She's going to be dashing to appointments for the next couple of weeks so I'm just letting you know that I might be a bit pushed.'

'Of course.' Molly gave a confused frown. 'You don't have to worry about upsetting me. I'm not that needy!'

'You're not needy at all.' He gave a wry smile, a look she couldn't quite interpret flicking over his features, but it faded before Molly could even attempt to read it. 'The thing is, I've cleared it with Rita, and Mum's going to drop the twins off at seven. I finish at eight, so they're *hopefully* going to amuse themselves in the playroom for an hour till I get off.'

'Great.' Molly beamed, but she could feel her heartbeat quickening, nervous somehow at the prospect of meeting Luke's children and desperately trying not to let it show. The children couldn't come into this, and it was important she keep things light, treat the fact he was bringing his children into work just as she would if it were any one of her colleagues. 'So what's the problem?'

'Problem?' Luke checked.

'You said you'd already cleared it with Rita.'

'I have.' Luke nodded. 'I just thought I should let you know—that you might feel a bit…' He gave a quick shake of his head. 'It doesn't matter.' As she turned to go he called her back. 'This weekend—you're off?'

'So are you.' Molly grinned, but it faded when she saw his expression.

'I don't think I'm going to be able to see you, Molly. I could maybe ask Mum if she can have the twins on Saturday night, only I seem to be asking her an awful lot, and I haven't really seen enough of the twins, with doing nights.'

'No problem.' Molly's smile snapped back on.

'But it's your birthday on Saturday.'

'How do you know…?' Molly frowned, because she deliberately hadn't told him. Deliberately, because birthdays and flowers and intimate dinners and celebrating milestones weren't what they were about.

'Some things you just remember. Look, I will try and arrange something.'

'There's really no need,' Molly said firmly. 'I've been neglecting my friends a bit of late. You enjoy the weekend with the kids.'

'Well, if you change your mind…' There was just a hint of emotion on his usually deadpan face. 'I mean, if you fancy kicking a ball around the park with the kids… then we could get a take-away or something…'

And it would be so, so easy to say yes—she was desperate for her days off and was really looking forward to catching up with her friends on Friday and hitting the shops, yet despite the smile, and despite the fact she'd played it down, it did matter that it was her birthday. It meant that this massive aching abyss wouldn't be filled till Monday. She wanted to see him, didn't want to wait till their shift ended on Tuesday morning, or till the kids were safely at kinder on Monday and he could knock at her door. Oh, she wanted him, wanted him in her bed, wanted to be in his, but she wanted more than that too.

It was Luke who broke the endless silence. Luke who drew the wrong conclusion when she didn't instantly respond. Luke who inadvertently saved her from herself. 'Am I right in thinking that footy's not really your thing?'

'These are the only flat shoes I own.' Molly clicked together her sensible navy nursing shoes. 'And I'm catching up with—'

'It's fine,' Luke interrupted. 'You don't need to explain your movements to me.'

Only she wanted to.

Wanted to be more important in his life as much as she wanted him to have a bigger place in hers.

Still, there wasn't time to dwell on it. By the time the ward was settled for the night Carl had arrived. Molly could hear him wheezing from the other end of the corridor as the paramedics wheeled him in.

'Young Carl.' The paramedic smiled as Molly approached. 'You're expecting him?'

'We are.' Molly smiled a welcome, but one glance at her new patient and she was reaching for the phone in her pocket. Carl was beyond being anxious, he was too exhausted with concentrating on his breathing to even notice his surroundings. Leaning forward on the stretcher, he was using his accessory muscles to breathe, and his eyes were closed, his whole body clearly drained from the exertion. This was one sick little boy, and the treatment room was the best place for him—all the equipment was to hand, and on a children's ward any procedures tended to be undertaken there so as to minimise distress to the other children, especially at night when hopefully the ward was sleeping.

'He's gone downhill in the ambulance...' The paramedic met Molly's eyes and she gave a brief nod. 'Let's pop him into the treatment room. Hello, Mrs Adams, I'm Molly, the nurse in charge tonight.'

'Where's the doctor?' Mrs Adams didn't return the greeting. 'I thought you were expecting us?'

"We are,' Molly responded. 'Dr Williams is over in Intensive Care at the moment. I'll let him know that you're here.'

'But he knew that we were coming.'

Two hours ago, Molly wanted to point out, tempted to tell Mrs Adams that her son wasn't the only patient under

Luke's care but knowing that the woman's rather brusque manner was probably masking her anxiety.

'Anything I can help with?' Anne Marie's face was welcome as she came into the treatment room.

'Could you settle Carl and take the handover from the paramedics?' Molly answered with just a hint of raised eyebrows as the phone trilled in her hand. 'I'm just going to let Doctor Williams know that his patient is here.'

'Carl Adams is here,' Molly said, stepping outside.

'How is he?'

'Not good,' Molly answered. 'We need you here.'

'I'm just in the middle—'

'Luke,' Molly interrupted, 'you accepted a direct admission.'

'His GP said—'

'I don't care what his GP said two hours ago,' Molly said crisply. 'I've got a seriously ill child just landed on my ward, and if he'd gone through Emergency he'd have been triaged to Resus—the emergency doctor would be seeing him, stat. We need you now.'

'I'm on my way.'

'Good,' Molly answered.

'Start him on some nebulised salbutamol.'

'I will, and can you arrange an urgent portable chest X-ray while you're running?'

Anne Marie had already set up the nebuliser. Normally Ventolin was given via a spacer, but Carl's air entry was poor and Molly spoke to Carl's mother as she replaced Carl's oxygen mask with the nebuliser and turned it on.

'Dr Wilson will be here in just a moment, Carl.' Molly helped him lean forward and placed a couple of pillows on his lap. 'Rest on these, that's a good boy. This medicine will start helping soon.' Anne Marie brought over the IV trolley and pulled out some local anaesthetic cream to numb his arm, but Molly shook her head. The cream took a while to work, and there was no point in telling Carl they were giving him cream to numb him before the needle when it wasn't going to have time to take effect.

'Hi, there, Carl.' Luke breezed in and set straight to work, taking a history from the mother as he slipped a tourniquet over Carl's thin arm.

'Carl, I'm just going to put a small needle into your arm. It's going to hurt just a bit, but I'll be as gentle as I can.'

'Are you taking some blood?' Mrs Adams asked.

'Yep, and we can get an IV started and give him some medicine. It will just be the one needle,' Luke reassured them both. 'I'm a pretty good aim.'

He was. Working in paediatrics, he was more than used to the tiny veins of the smallest of babies, but even so Carl barely grimaced as the needle went in, which was worrying. 'We'll need IV hydrocortisone. When did he start his prednisolone?' Luke asked Carl's mother.

'I'm sorry?' Mrs Adams was concentrating on her son.

'Your GP said he started him on a reducing course of prednisolone on Wednesday. When did he have his last dose? I need to work out how much to give him.'

'Is it really necessary?' Mrs Adams gave an agitated shake of her head. 'He's on the nebuliser. He's already had two courses of steroids in the last couple of months.'

'Mrs Adams.' Luke's voice was calm and even, but there was absolutely no doubt of the seriousness of his question. 'Is your son on the medication your GP pre-scribed him?'

'He gave me a script and said that if it got worse…' Her voice trailed off for a moment, and Luke did nothing to fill the silence except stare over at the boy struggling to breathe. 'He wasn't like this!' Mrs Adams insisted. 'He actually seemed a bit better, but when he got worse this evening I was going to go and get the prescription dis-pensed. I don't like him to have steroids. I'm aware what the side effects are.'

Luke didn't even deign to give a response, just called his orders to Molly and administered the essential steroids, all the while talking in reassuring tones to Carl, whose breathing was starting to get a little easier with the cocktail of drugs being delivered via the nebuliser. The radiographer arrived to do a portable X-ray.

'Any chance you could be pregnant?' he asked Molly as he handed her the heavy lead gown. Carl was too ill to be left alone and needed some reassurance and support to sit up and hold his breath while the X-ray was taken.

'No, none,' Molly answered automatically, pulling the heavy gown over her head.

'Actually, I'll stay with him.' Luke took the gown from her. 'Molly, could you ring the nurse-co-ordinator? There aren't any ICU beds. You'll need to let her know that unless he picks up soon, I'm going to have to arrange a transfer.'

It made perfect sense. In fact, transfer or no transfer, she needed an extra nurse out on the ward floor or an ex-perienced nurse to stay with Carl, as his sudden arrival had spread the ward staff thinly and already the routine was falling behind. But Luke had given her a look as she'd taken the gown—just that tiny frown at her carelessness—because until she got her period Luke wouldn't think she was out of the woods.

As Molly headed out of the room there was an uneasy wobble in her throat, a realisation that even if she hadn't outright lied to Luke, she hadn't told the truth.

Hadn't let the man who was closest to her in on the painful truth. It had seemed right at the time—right not to burden him with it.

Only now…

Now somehow she wished that she had.

'Are you OK?' Anne Marie frowned at her pensive face.

'Fine.' Molly nodded, picking up the telephone and putting her personal problems firmly aside.

'This is one sick kid.' Luke's face was grim when he came out of the treatment room. 'What the hell was his mother thinking?'

'I've no idea,' Molly replied. 'I've spoken to the nursing supervisor and she's going to send me a nurse from HDU. Do you still want him to have aminophylline?'

'Not yet.' Luke wrote up his orders on the drug sheet. 'Hopefully he'll start picking up now that he's getting the right medication. For now he needs hourly nebs, but if he doesn't improve soon I'm going to have to transfer him,' Luke said grimly. 'I'm going to talk to the mother.'

'I'll come with you.'

Luke took a long and detailed history from the mother, listening without comment at first when she explained her reasons for not giving the medication.

'He only gets asthma during hay-fever season. Last

year they gave him three lots of steroids and this year he's already had two. I just think the doctor hands out the script automatically. I just thought it better to hold off— to see if he improved without them.'

'Why?'

'Because I'm aware of the side-effects.'

'Such as?' Luke frowned.

'Well, it can affect their growth,' Mrs Adams said. 'And Carl's a bit on the short side.'

'Are you aware of the side-effects if he doesn't have them?' Luke asked, and Molly watched Mrs Adams's face tighten. 'Are you aware how sick your son is tonight—that if he doesn't improve in the next couple of hours, or if he deteriorates any further, he's going to have to be transferred to an intensive care bed?'

'I honestly thought I was helping.' Mrs Adams's face crumpled, but Luke's didn't—and because she knew him, Molly knew he was angry. A muscle was leaping in his cheek, his shoulders rigid as he stared coolly at the woman in front of him. 'I just thought if we held off, if I upped his puffers, he'd be OK.'

'If,' Luke said crisply, 'you believe your doctor is over-prescribing, or you don't have faith in him, I suggest you look around for another doctor you can discuss your concerns with, one you feel comfortable with. Do *that*, Mrs Adams, before you start practising internet medicine or testing your theories on your son.'

'I will.' Clearly shaken, Mrs Adams stood up. 'Can I go and sit with him?'

'Of course,' Molly said. 'We're going to keep him in

the treatment room for now, where all the equipment is, with a nurse specialling him. I'll take you down to him.'

Luke was still in his office when she came back, his anger still palpable—and he was right to be angry, right to be frustrated, but it was *how* angry he was that concerned Molly. Not white-hot, raging angry, and most wouldn't have even picked up on it, only Molly could feel it.

'Luke—'

'Stupid, stupid woman.' Luke's mouth twisted on the words. 'I don't know whether to report her.'

'She made a mistake,' Molly pointed out.

'And if she makes it again, it could cost her son's life.'

'I think she got that message.'

'What—you think I was too hard on her?'

'No!' Molly shook her head. 'She needed to be told and she was. I don't think she'll play with his health again. But maybe you should discuss it with her GP—or your consultant. Luke…' She was genuinely concerned. They'd sat in this very room with child abusers, had had to listen to the most heinous of things—but his reaction today was extreme. 'Is there something I'm missing here?'

'Like what?' he snapped.

'Well, we all have our buttons,' Molly said slowly, 'and this seems to be yours. Do the twins have asthma?'

'This has nothing to do with the twins, Molly!' Luke glared past her shoulder, then took a deep breath, the anger seeping out of him. 'I'm fine.'

'You're sure?'

'Sure.' He gave a pale smile. 'I'll talk to her again in

the morning. I'll go over his asthma plan with her and make sure she's got the message.'

Which he did—only it was Mrs Adams who instigated it.

By seven a.m. Carl was on the main ward, with the nurse special back in her own ward.

'How are you doing?' Luke listened carefully to his chest. 'That sounds a lot better.'

'I feel a lot better.'

'He's tired.' Mrs Adams gave a worried frown. 'He really hasn't slept much.'

'He'll soon catch up on that. We'll probably keep him here over the weekend, just to make sure we're on top of it.'

'Actually, Doctor…' Mrs Adams cleared her throat. 'I was wondering if I could have a word.' She barely got to the ward door before she burst into tears. 'I feel so stupid. I had no idea how bad he'd get.'

'Come on,' Luke said kindly. 'We'll go in my office and have a talk.' He glanced at his watch. 'Er, Molly…'

'No problem.' Molly smiled, but her heart was fluttering at the prospect of meeting his kids. 'I'll keep an eye on them.'

CHAPTER EIGHT

THE office door hadn't even closed before they arrived.

Mrs Williams was holding the twins firmly by the hands, as if she expected them to suddenly run off, as Molly introduced herself.

They were gorgeous.

Blond-haired and blue-eyed, they didn't say a word as Molly led the trio to the playroom. 'You're to sit here and you're not to disturb the staff!' Mrs Williams said sternly to her grandchildren, who were sitting on the sofa, both washed and dressed, Amelia with a pair of fairy wings, and little backpacks at their feet and looking just adorable.

Luke was definitely his mother's son—tall, her blonde hair now streaked with silver, with the strong features that worked better on a male, she was certainly quite a formidable-looking woman, but her eyes were kind.

'I'm terribly sorry to impose!'

'It's not a problem,' Molly assured her, then turned to the twins, who were staring at their feet. 'Your dad's just with a patient at the moment, but he knows that you're here and will try and come along soon. If you need anything, just ask. They'll be fine,' Molly added to the rather anxious Mrs Williams.

'Oh, *they'll* be fine,' Mrs Williams said, after kissing the children and walking with Molly back out to the ward. 'It's your playroom I'm worried about! They may look as if butter wouldn't melt but they can be a couple of little minxes. They're way too used to running wild.'

Which Molly doubted—Luke was so insistent on respect and good manners, and Molly could now see where it came from. Mrs Williams really was an imposing woman and no doubt ran a tight ship. 'Again, I really do apologise for the inconvenience.'

'Happens all the time!' Molly said cheerfully, walking her out of the ward. Well, maybe not *all* the time, but a staff member's child sitting in the playroom, waiting for their parent to finish their shift wasn't a unique occurrence on the children's ward, though usually it was their mother they were waiting for, and that fact alone meant that the staff would give them just a little bit more fuss than usual.

'What are they like?' Anne Marie asked, coming out of the kitchen with a baby bottle.

'Gorgeous,' Molly said. 'Come and say hi!'

Only the two little angels she'd left sitting not two minutes ago seemed to have left the building—toys were everywhere, the television blaring, Amelia jumping up and down on the sofa as Angus sped around on a tricycle that was way too small for him.

'Hey, guys…' Anne Marie barked over the noise of the television. 'Time to settle down.'

'You talk funny!' Amelia giggled, jumping up and down on the sofa. 'Doesn't she, Angus?'

'Yeah.' Angus zoomed the tricycle to a stop. 'You talk funny!'

'Gorgeous!' Anne Marie rolled her eyes. 'And such lovely manners, too!'

Anne Marie, in fact, ended up feeding her patient in the playroom so she could keep an eye on the twins. The other nurses watched the ward while Molly gave handover to the day staff, which took for ever as Rita had been off for two days and didn't know most of the patients.

'How's Bernadette's mood?'

'She's perked up,' Molly said. 'She's getting on well with young Nathan, so she's got a friend now, but it's the school disco this weekend, apparently—she really feels she's missing out.'

'She is missing out,' Rita sighed. 'She's been here for weeks now.'

'And that one!' Anne Marie was giving her orders, and the playroom was a lot tidier by the time Molly came back. 'Go on, put it back in the toy box!'

'Ready for the off?' Molly grinned.

'Am I ever. I just want to ring John before I go, though— Oh, hi, Luke.'

'Daddy!' Two squeals of delight went up and the twins hurled themselves at him.

'How have they been?' Luke asked. 'Not too much trouble, I hope?'

'They were great.' Anne Marie beamed through gritted teeth. 'Full of beans!'

'Well, thank you.' Luke gripped the twins' hands tightly as he headed off, and this time Molly knew why.

With Anne Marie ringing her husband, Molly walked out with Luke.

'How was Mrs Adams?' Molly asked.

'Good.' Luke nodded. 'I've handed it over to Tom, and I'm sure it won't happen again—she just didn't realise how serious it could get. I've gone over everything with her, and in fairness I don't think her GP really had explained things very well. She had no real idea about peak-flow recordings and how important they were.' Luke held onto the twins rather than smother the loud yawn that hit him.

'Are you going to get any sleep?'

'Nope…' Luke yawned again. 'Not till Mum gets back from her appointment.'

'What about kinder?' Molly asked, then answered her own question. 'Oh, that's right, they don't have it on Friday. Will you be OK for work tonight?'

'I'll have to be!'

'Luke…' They were at the car park, his eyes so red it looked as if he'd been swimming in chlorine. She actually opened her mouth to offer to come over and watch them till his mum got back. After all, she didn't have to work tonight—it made perfect sense, what any friend would do…

'What?' He was holding two little hands in one big one as he fumbled in his pocket for his car keys.

'Oh, nothing… See you, then.'

'See you, Molly.'

'See you, guys!'

And it was as much of a goodbye as they could have with the twins there. Only it hurt, actually felt wrong to be walking away when she didn't want to. To know she wouldn't see Luke till Monday, to know he was exhausted and she could do something to help.

But that meant crossing the line.

That meant getting involved.

And that was something she *needed* to think carefully about.

There was nothing as bleak as a post-divorce birthday.

There was nothing as bleak as letting yourself in at five minutes past midnight to a house that was empty and a husband that was no longer there.

Oh, she'd been a sister doing it for herself tonight, had wiggled her bum on the dance floor and sworn she'd survive along with the rest of the crowd.

And she would.

Holding her cat to her chest, even though he was scratching to get out, Molly knew that she would survive. Glimpsed that day in the long way-off future, when she'd bump into Richard and his rapidly growing brood and be able to smile.

Molly stared at the wall, at the silly crystals she'd hung to promote new energy, held onto her cat, who was purring now, and hated it that she was alone on her birthday.

It wasn't age she feared, and it wasn't loneliness—just that horrible thought that you might die in bed alone. Unnoticed for days. That you weren't worth checking on, Molly thought melodramatically. But it was ten minutes into her birthday so she was allowed to be, Molly decided, because next year she'd be thirty.

Which had her reaching for the tissues.

And she knew people cared. Molly blew loudly into her tissue.

She knew she'd be missed before the neighbours noticed a pong.

Rolling on her side, Molly hugged her cat closer.

She knew that she mattered.

Only it wasn't the same.

'Good that there aren't kids involved.'

Everyone said it—her lawyer, her family, her friends, even Luke.

And she wasn't being melodramatic any more, just very, very sad and terribly honest…

With herself.

Because, yes, she smiled and nodded, almost right to the point she agreed—only this horrible, selfish part of her didn't.

She *wanted* there to have been kids involved and pictures on her fridge, to be yawning at work because the kids wouldn't let her sleep, wanted to moan that her boobs were no more. Was sick of working over Christmas because apparently she didn't need to be home on Christmas morning.

But she wanted to be there so badly that it really was a need.

A need Richard had had too—a need that had pushed Molly to look at adoption.

But he'd wanted his own children, which meant that he hadn't wanted her—and she didn't want him any more either. She wanted Luke—only she didn't want his kids…

'Why do men snore?' Anne-Marie's warm Scottish voice on the end of the phone pierced her loneliness.

'Why does every man I fall in love with go and get someone else pregnant?'

'There's no answer to either,' Anne Marie sighed. 'I rang a few times, so don't think you've got a load of messages! Oh, and I've decided that we're getting next-door flats in the retirement village,' she continued, pretending she couldn't hear her friend's tears. "We'll drink lots of gin and cheat at bingo and you can flirt with all the rich retirees!'

'I'm not worried about getting old.'

'Well, I am, and just in case you are, I'm letting you know that we've got a plan! Happy birthday, Molly.'

CHAPTER NINE

'HAPPY birthday!'

Blinking at her front door, her dressing-gown wrapped around her, Molly tried to work out what day it was.

She'd been out with friends last night, Friday night, and then Anne Marie had rung. Luke had been working, but he was off for the weekend now…which meant it was Saturday morning, Molly realised.

And she was still alive!

Very early in the morning, actually, and Luke was standing in her doorway, dressed in scrubs, in desperate need of a shave and holding…

'Here!' He handed her a massive bunch of flowers— not roses, which was good, because they weren't her favourite. Instead he'd brought a massive bunch of pale pink lilies, which *were* her favourite—especially when they came with lots of carefully arranged twigs sticking out, especially when they were being held out by a gorgeous specimen of a man.

'I'm assuming you didn't get these at the local garage.' Molly buried her face in them and no doubt came out with a yellow nose. 'And I don't think the local florist opens